12

S0-BCI-561

A Long Way Home

Mysteries of Sparrow Island™

A LONG WAY HOME

Kristin Eckhardt

Guideposts Books
CARMEL, NEW YORK

Huntington City Township
Public Library
200 West Market Street
Huntington, IN 46750

Mysteries of Sparrow Island is a trademark of Guideposts.

Copyright © 2006 by Guideposts, Carmel, New York 10512.
All rights reserved.

No part of this publication may be reproduced, stored in a
retrieval system or transmitted in any form or by any means,
electronic, mechanical, photocopying, recording or otherwise,
without the written permission of the publisher. Inquiries
should be addressed to the Rights & Permissions Department,
Guideposts, 16 E. 34th St., New York, NY 10016.

All Scripture quotations are taken from *The Holy Bible, New
International Version.* Copyright © 1973, 1978, 1984 International
Bible Society. Used by permission of Zondervan Bible Publishers.

www.guideposts.org
(800) 431-2344   —
Guideposts Books & Inspirational Media Division

Cover and interior design by Cindy LaBreacht
Cover art by Gail W. Guth
Map by Jim Haynes, represented by Creative Freelancers, Inc.
Typeset by Nancy Tardi
Printed in the United States of America

With love to my dad,
Wayne Knudsen.

TO U.S.A.

ORCAS

LUMMI

N
W E
S

CYPRESS

GUEMES

TO ANACORTES

FIDALGO ISLAND

*SPARROW ISLAND IS FICTITIOUS

CHAPTER ❦ ONE

I SHOULD HAVE GONE INTO training," Abby Stanton gasped as she scrambled up the steep path. She was doing her best to keep up with Iona Benson, a seventy-year-old power walker who had competed in races all across the country.

Now it seemed the woman was trying to break the speed record for the fastest tour on Sparrow Island—a tour that Abby was supposed to be leading if she could ever catch up with Iona.

When they reached the top of the hill, Iona checked the stopwatch hanging from her neck, then flashed a triumphant smile in Abby's direction. "We're three minutes and fifty-eight seconds ahead of schedule. Good job! Most of my tour guides give up after the first mile or two."

Abby paused a moment to catch her breath. As an ornithologist, she did a lot of hiking and considered herself in good physical condition. She'd just never led a tour at such a breakneck pace before.

Abby was glad she'd agreed to give Iona a private birding tour. If any other tourists had come along, they might have staged a mutiny. She tugged at the neckline of her khaki birding vest, feeling overly warm from the brisk walk.

Iona adjusted the red ball cap she wore to protect her face from the rays of the bright June sun. A fringe of white curls peeked from beneath the brim and her brown eyes sparkled with curiosity as she looked around the clearing.

"This is beautiful," Iona exclaimed. "So peaceful."

Abby took a deep breath of the clean, fresh air, the fragrant pine mingling with the scent of brine from the nearby sound. A light breeze cooled her brow and fleecy white clouds floated lazily in the blue sky above them.

Abby pulled a small canteen of water from her vest and offered it to Iona. "Would you like a drink?"

The older woman shook her head. "No, thank you. Water slows me down. I'll re-hydrate after the race . . . I mean, the tour." She checked her stopwatch. "We only have eighteen minutes and thirty-four seconds left on the clock."

Abby tipped the canteen up to her mouth and took a long drink, grateful that she'd packed it along on this mild Friday morning. She loved the temperate climate of the San Juan Islands, never too hot in the summer or too cold in the winter. Certainly nothing like New York, where she'd lived for the last thirty-five years working as a researcher at Cornell University's Lab of Ornithology. Now that she'd moved back home, she didn't miss the freezing blizzards in the winter or the sweltering days of summer.

A thunderstorm had rocked Sparrow Island last night, but this morning had dawned clear and bright. Abby took another drink from the canteen, the cool water refreshing her considerably. Then she capped the canteen and tucked it back into her vest, ready to resume the tour.

"Now, where are the ospreys?" Iona asked, her gaze scanning the trees surrounding them.

Abby pointed down the hill toward a tall fir tree. "There, on the third branch from the top. Can you see the nest?"

Iona pulled a pair of binoculars from the blue canvas knapsack that matched her jogging suit. "Ah, yes," she said, peering through the binoculars. "I think I see it."

Abby moved beside her, reaching for her own binoculars. She'd found this spot a month ago, the top of the hill providing a perfect vantage point to view activity inside the nest.

"It's so big," Iona said. "Why, it must be three feet in diameter."

"Can you see the two chicks in there?" Abby asked.

Iona adjusted her binoculars. "Yes, I see them. Oh, aren't they cute? They don't even have feathers yet."

"They won't start to fledge for another week or so," Abby informed her. "The chicks will stay near the nest with their parents until October. Then they'll be ready to fly off on their own."

"They're just darling," Iona crooned, then pointed toward the sky. "Oh . . . look at that!"

Abby smiled as an adult osprey circled above them, a small fish hanging from its talons. "It must be lunchtime."

"Is that the mother or the father?" Iona asked, her voice subdued in wonder as the bird gracefully descended into the nest.

"The mother," Abby replied. "You can't always tell, but some females, like this one, have a ring of dark feathers around the neck."

"Ospreys look similar to eagles, don't they?"

"Some people get the two confused," Abby replied, "but ospreys are smaller and have brown and white tail feathers. Mature eagles have entirely white tails and heads."

"This is all so interesting." Iona lowered her binoculars. "And I'd love to hear more, but I'm afraid it's time to move on."

"But there's a pileated woodpecker over here," Abby told her, moving to the opposite side of the path. "Can you hear it?"

"Yes, I can . . ." Iona took a step in that direction, then paused to look at her stopwatch. "But I do like to keep on time."

"It will only take a moment." Abby pointed to a tree in the distance. "The hole it makes to roost is very distinct—it's in the shape of a rectangle."

"A rectangular hole?" Iona moved next to her and peered through her binoculars. "Well, so it is. Amazing!"

Abby scanned the trees with her binoculars. "And there's a western tanager that's nesting on five eggs. They're due to hatch any day now."

"No time for tanagers, I'm afraid." Iona turned and began heading back down the path. "I'm supposed to tour The Nature Museum in exactly twelve minutes and twenty-nine seconds. Then it's off to Friday Harbor for a kayaking expedition."

Abby raced after her, disappointed that Iona insisted on sticking to her tight schedule. She enjoyed sharing her knowledge of birds with people and could tell Iona truly appreciated it, just not quite as much as she appreciated her stopwatch.

"You're certainly very punctual," Abby observed, pumping her arms and legs in conjunction with Iona.

The older woman chuckled. "That comes from having worked at Union Station in Chicago for thirty years. We had to keep the trains on time. I suppose I got used to planning my personal life on a timetable too."

It always intrigued Abby to learn the backgrounds of the people who visited the islands. Many of the tourists seemed equally curious about her, often envying her position as the Associate Curator at the Sparrow Island Nature Conservatory and the opportunities she had to work with wildlife on a daily basis.

Abby knew she sometimes took the blessings in her own life for granted. Like Iona, she didn't always take the time to appreciate her surroundings.

She slowed her stride, letting Iona forge ahead as she composed a silent prayer, thanking God for all the gifts He had given her. For bringing her back home to Sparrow Island and her family after her sister Mary's car accident. And for giving her the opportunity to view the beauty of His creation every day.

"Nothing irritates me more than a glitch in my schedule," Iona continued, waiting for Abby to catch up with her. "I was supposed to go whale-watching this afternoon, but my tour was cancelled. Such a shame, really. I so wanted to see the orcas while I was here. I have to leave for home early tomorrow morning."

"Surely there are other tour boats going out to view the orcas this afternoon," Abby said, lengthening her stride. "Perhaps you can get a ticket on one of them."

She knew it might not be easy without an advance reservation. This was the prime season for whale-watching. As a girl, Abby had loved going out on her father's charter boat to view the orcas, also known as killer whales. She'd even gotten to know the orca pods so well that she could recognize individual members.

A pod was an extended family group made up of twenty to sixty whales. There were three pods of resident orcas that lived in the waters between the San Juan Islands and Vancouver. They were known simply as the J pod, the K pod and the L Pod.

In 1976, researchers began keeping track of the orcas by giving each one an identification number and a name according to their distinct markings. Abby knew that each pod was closely monitored for any change in the population resulting from a birth or a death.

While the orcas were the favorites of many tourists, there was a wide variety of marine life around the islands. Minke whales, gray whales, porpoises, seals and sea lions, just to name a few.

Iona shook her head. "All of the whale-watching tours have been cancelled today. Apparently, one of the orcas was injured last night and the entire pod disrupted."

"Injured?" Abby hadn't heard this disturbing news. "How did that happen?"

"No one knows for certain," Iona replied. "But I heard that foul play is suspected. Apparently, the injury was quite severe. Some people just have no respect for animals or the environment."

Foul play? The words echoed in Abby's head. That didn't make any sense. Who would purposely hurt one of those magnificent orcas?

Iona checked her stopwatch, then increased her pace. "I'm afraid there's no more time for dilly-dallying. Let's hop to it!"

Abby followed after her, still worried about the injured orca. She cared about all the wildlife on the islands, believing it was important to follow God's charge to exercise good stewardship over the earth.

She just hoped there was something she could do to help.

ABBY SOUGHT OUT HER BOSS, Hugo Baron, as soon as she returned to The Nature Museum. She found him in his office, writing in the journal that he'd kept for years. Hugo and his late wife had traveled the world before her death. Then he'd settled on Sparrow Island, and founded the conservatory and The Nature Museum.

His journal must be filled with all kinds of adventures, Abby thought to herself as she stood in the open doorway, not wanting to interrupt him. He often said it helped him to reflect on his life by keeping a record of the joys and heartaches he'd experienced in his sixty-five years.

Abby wondered if he ever mentioned her in his journal, then felt her face flush as Hugo looked up from his desk.

"Oh, hello, Abby. I didn't see you there."

She hesitated in the doorway. "I didn't mean to disturb you."

Hugo closed the journal, then stood up and flashed a wide smile. "Not at all. Please come in."

Abby felt rumpled after her brisk tour with Mrs. Benson, especially when she noticed Hugo's dapper attire. He wore a dove gray suit and a pale blue tie that matched his eyes. She put a hand up to her hair and found a small twig there.

"Looks like I brought home a souvenir from my tour with Iona Benson," Abby quipped, tucking the twig into a vest pocket. She'd take it to the laboratory later, knowing it could be recycled as nest building material in the future.

"I saw the two of you leave earlier," Hugo said. "I didn't envy you trying to keep up with that woman."

"She competes in racewalking competitions, and I'm afraid I came in last today," Abby replied. "But I do feel invigorated." She took a chair opposite his desk. "Have you heard about the injured orca?"

His smile faded. "Yes, I spoke to a zoologist at Lopez Island about half an hour ago. The orca's name is Rosie and she's from the K pod."

"Is she all right?"

"I'm afraid Rosie beached herself early this morning."

"Oh no." Abby gasped. "Then the injury must be serious."

Hugo nodded. "She has a broken dorsal fin and a gaping wound right next to it."

"How did that happen?"

"Due to the nature of the injuries, it appears she was rammed by a large boat sometime last night."

Abby shuddered at the thought that someone could be so careless. An adult orca would be hard to miss. No, *impossible* to miss. "Will Rosie be all right?"

"Yes, that's the good news. They sutured her wounds, then towed her back near K pod. She seems to be recovering. The bad news is that she has a six-month-old calf named Poppy that's now missing."

Abby stared at him in disbelief. "Missing?"

"I'm afraid so," Hugo replied. "The zoologist said that as soon as they identified Rosie, they sent out a boat to check on the rest of the K pod. All of the orcas were accounted for except Rosie's calf."

"Oh no," Abby exclaimed.

"Poppy must have gotten disoriented when the boat that

injured her mother sailed through the pod. We don't know yet if Poppy was injured, too, or possibly even killed."

Abby's heart ached for the missing orca calf. "Why would a boat captain get so close to an orca pod, much less slice right through it? Who would do such a thing?"

Hugo sighed. "Someone too selfish to care. The danger is that he, or she, may do it again."

A knock at the door interrupted their conversation and they both turned to see a young man in his mid-twenties standing in the open doorway. His sun-kissed blond hair was slightly curled at the ends and hung almost to his shoulders. His face was deeply tanned and his eyes were the color of the ocean.

"Hello," he began, "I'm looking for Dr. Stanton and I'm hoping you might be able to help me find her."

"Look no further," Hugo replied, waving him inside. "She's right here."

The young man smiled when he saw Abby. "Dr. Stanton?"

"Yes," she replied, rising to her feet, "I'm Abby Stanton."

He reached out to shake her hand. "My name is Mick Wymore. I must say that Dr. Sima described you perfectly."

"You know Lauren Sima?" Abby said, already feeling a bond with the young man. Lauren had been one of her dearest friends back at Cornell University, as well as a fellow professor. They'd often spent their summer breaks hiking together in the Adirondacks.

"I do indeed, Dr. Stanton. I did my graduate work at Cornell."

"Please call me Abby," she said.

He nodded. "All right, if you'll call me Mick. Dr. Sima made me promise that I'd look you up when I reached the San Juan Islands to start my doctoral research."

"But I thought Lauren was on a teaching sabbatical in Greece."

"She was heading there when I left but she's probably back at Cornell by now," Mick replied. "It's taken me a while to get here. I decided to take a little vacation and sailed by way of the Galapagos Islands before heading to the Pacific Northwest."

Abby turned to Hugo, not wanting to leave him out of the conversation. "Mick, this is the Curator of the Sparrow Island Nature Conservatory, Hugo Baron."

"Nice to meet you." Mick reached out to shake his hand.

"How did you like the Galapagos Islands?" Hugo asked him. "That's one of my favorite places in the world."

"It was absolutely fascinating," Mick agreed. "I spent much longer there than I intended, but there was so much to see."

"What field are you in?" Abby asked him.

"I'm a marine biologist. I grew up on the coast of Maine and consider the ocean my second home, so it seemed like a natural career choice."

"Indeed," Hugo agreed. "Welcome to the San Juan Islands. Although I'm afraid you've come at a troubling time."

Mick's brow furrowed as he looked between the two of them. "Is there a problem?"

"We just found out that a boat rammed a mother orca last night and disrupted the K pod," Abby explained. "Now her six-month-old calf, Poppy, is missing."

Anger flashed in Mick's deep blue eyes. "How could that happen?"

"We don't know," Abby said. "But we need to find out who's responsible so that it doesn't happen again."

"In the meantime, we're worried about the calf," Hugo said. "The Coast Guard is investigating the incident, but their main focus is on finding the culprit, not the missing baby orca. I don't know how long Poppy can survive without her mother or the rest of the K pod."

"That is a concern," Mick agreed, "as well as an amazing coincidence. The subject of my doctoral research is the socialization habits of orcas. If we can reunite Poppy with her mother, it could help us understand how the orcas form their strong family bonds with each other."

Abby had loved the orcas since she was a child and knew they were very close-knit, social whales who lived in the same pod their entire lives.

"I hope we can reunite them." Hugo sighed. "Unfortunately, we don't even know for certain if Poppy is still alive."

"But we can't give up hope," Abby said. "Not while there's still a chance."

"Maybe I can help," Mick offered. "I'm supposed to evaluate each of the pods this afternoon. I've spent the last couple of weeks here familiarizing myself with the orca pods and their movements. Do you happen to know where this incident occurred?"

Hugo walked over to his desk and picked up a notepad. "The zoologist I talked to earlier said it must have happened a few miles off of Lopez Island. That's where the K pod was seen yesterday. Rosie, the mother orca, beached herself on the west shore of Lopez Island."

Mick paled. "Beached whales don't often survive. What's her condition?"

"She's actually doing very well," Hugo said. "They treated her wounds and towed her back near the pod. The other orcas are taking care of her now."

"Those strong family ties are what makes the orcas so

fascinating," Mick said. "And why it's imperative that the missing calf is reunited with them as soon as possible."

"We'd appreciate any help you can offer," Abby told him.

Mick looked thoughtful. "Perhaps I'll focus on the area around the K pod for today and evaluate the other pods later." He glanced at his watch. "In fact, there's no reason I can't get started right now. I'll check in with the director of The Whale Museum first so we can coordinate our efforts."

Abby breathed a sigh of relief. "That would be so helpful. I've done search-and-rescue—though for people, not orcas—and time is of the essence."

Mick headed toward the door. "I'll get right on it."

Abby followed him. "Please let us know what you find out."

"I'll probably be out most of the day—at least until dark," Mick replied. "Why don't I stop in here first thing in the morning?"

"Thank you, Mick," Abby said, then watched him walk briskly down the hallway.

Hugo joined her at the door. "He seems like a fine young man. How fortunate that he showed up here today."

"Yes, it is." Abby sent up a silent prayer for his safety as he conducted the search. "I just wish I could do more to help."

"Perhaps you can." Hugo stroked his white mustache, deep in thought. "When I talked to the man who treated Rosie, he told me the Coast Guard is asking for help in the investigation. Discovering who committed this crime on the open water is going to be extremely difficult."

She nodded. "I agree."

"What kind of boat would be the most likely to cut through one of the orca pods?"

Abby thought about his question for a moment. "One large enough not to be destroyed when it collided with an adult orca."

"Which means it probably wasn't a pleasure boat," Hugo mused.

"No," Abby said. "Something larger. Like one of the whale-watching tour boats."

Hugo nodded. "That makes the most sense. Specifically, those boats that take tours near the K pod every day."

Anticipation shot through Abby. "I could interview the captains of those boats tomorrow. Perhaps one of them might know something."

"Good idea," Hugo replied. "Take all the time you need. It's not going to be easy to find who was responsible."

Abby knew he was right, but she wouldn't let that stop her—not until she'd investigated every possible lead.

As a good steward, she could do no less.

CHAPTER ✿ TWO

That evening, Abby walked into the house she shared with her sister and inhaled the savory aroma of a meatloaf cooking in the oven. She wasn't overly fond of meatloaf, but Mary was such a talented cook that Abby's mouth watered in anticipation nonetheless. She'd worked up an appetite during her power walk this morning and she hoped dinner would be ready soon.

The kitchen table was set, with a beautiful bouquet of fresh flowers gracing the center, but Abby didn't see any sign of her sister. Placing her bag on the kitchen counter, Abby went in search of her. She checked Mary's craft room and bedroom, but found them both empty. The white van Mary drove was parked in the driveway, and Abby knew her sister wouldn't leave home with food in the oven.

"Mary?" she called out.

But there was no answer.

As Abby walked through the house she noted that Finnegan was nowhere in sight, either. The loyal service dog, a yellow Labrador and golden retriever mix, rarely left Mary's side.

When she reached the living room, Abby saw Blossom, the snow white Persian cat, grooming herself on the armchair. Blossom looked unconcerned about the missing Mary and Finnegan, but Abby was becoming more puzzled by the minute.

Then she saw a glimpse of her sister's wheelchair through the window and breathed a sigh of relief. She should have known Mary would be out tending the flowers in her garden, since she'd inherited the green thumb in the family.

Abby walked to the sliding glass door and pulled it open, the heady scent of geraniums greeting her. The bright red blooms spilled out of the planter next to the door. She stepped outside just as Mary rounded the corner of the house.

"Hello, Abby. I didn't hear you drive up."

"I just got home a few minutes ago." Abby walked over to join her sister on the lawn. She noticed the dog's harness hanging loosely from the arm of Mary's wheelchair. "Where's Finnegan?"

"I'm not really sure." Mary's brow crinkled as she looked around the yard. "He seems to have disappeared. You know how he likes to play fetch with his tennis ball?"

Abby nodded, having worn her arm out many a time throwing that old yellow tennis ball around the yard for Finnegan to chase.

"Well," Mary continued, brushing a stray rose petal off her apron, "I was doing some pruning and he kept bringing the tennis ball for me to throw. I really let it sail the last time and it must have landed somewhere in those bushes over there."

She pointed to the purple lilacs and lush pink rhododendrons lining the weathered cedar fence that separated the back yard from the woods. "That was five minutes ago and I haven't seen him since."

That was unusual. While Finnegan enjoyed playing in the backyard, he always stuck close by Mary in case she needed him.

"Do you suppose he got lost in there?" Abby asked. "Or distracted by a ground squirrel or something?"

"I don't know, but he's been gone long enough that I think we should go check it out." Mary turned her wheelchair and started toward the fence.

Abby walked beside her, breathing in the fragrant bouquet of the flowers. Mary's talent with plants had made the backyard resplendent with a wide variety of colors and scents that would grace the yard throughout the summer and into autumn.

"I'm not sure which smells better," Abby said, "the meatloaf cooking in the kitchen or all the flowers blooming out here."

Mary laughed. "You've never been a big fan of meatloaf, so you must be hungry."

"I'm starving," Abby admitted. "I led a tour with a woman who participates in racewalking competitions and likes to live by her stopwatch. I spent most of the time trying to keep up with her and definitely worked up an appetite."

"Dinner will be ready in a few minutes," Mary promised.

Abby's mind wandered to the missing orca calf, wondering if Poppy would be able to forage for food on her own. Probably not. Especially if she was hurt. Or in shock from losing her family.

"What's wrong?" Mary asked, ever perceptive to Abby's moods. It was just another sign of how close the sisters had grown since Abby had moved back to Sparrow Island.

"Have you heard about the injured orca?"

Mary nodded. "Henry mentioned it when he called me this afternoon."

Sgt. Henry Cobb was Mary's beau, as well as the San Juan County deputy sheriff. He not only doted on her sister, but made her laugh and for that alone Abby would have liked him. Henry was a kind, decent man with a calming air of authority that earned the respect of the people around him.

"He told me the orca's calf is missing too," Mary continued.

"I can't stop thinking about the baby orca," Abby told her, "all alone in the water without her mother or family to care for her."

"Is it true that a boat cut through the K pod?" Mary asked.

Abby nodded. "That's the only explanation that makes sense, although as far as I know there aren't any witnesses."

"I don't understand it." Mary's wheelchair rolled easily over the smooth, flat lawn. "How could anyone not notice colliding with a six-ton killer whale? And if they did notice it, why didn't they come forward so Rosie could get help right away?"

"Fear, maybe," Abby mused, "or they just didn't care."

Mary shook her head. Neither of them understood that kind of mindset. Their parents had raised them to respect nature and everything in God's universe.

A loud bark sounded in the distance, making Abby and Mary exchange glances.

"That's Finnegan," Mary said. "Finnegan! Come here, boy."

The dog responded with another series of barks.

"It sounds like he's on the other side of the fence," Abby said.

"But how could he be?" Mary asked her. "The fence is too high for him to jump over."

Abby walked along the cedar fence line, wading through the bushes until she saw a rift at the bottom of the panels where the wood had rotted away.

"This is how," she called out to Mary. "The tennis ball must have rolled through this hole and Finnegan somehow managed to squeeze himself through here to go after it."

Affection lit Mary's blue eyes. "Now he probably can't get back inside. Poor Finnegan."

On cue, the dog began barking again.

"At least he's calling for help." Abby moved behind the wheelchair and steered her sister toward the small gate that was almost hidden behind the thick line of bushes. The path was rougher here, making the going a little bumpy.

"I think I need shock absorbers on this thing," Mary quipped when the chair bounced over a rut.

"Just be glad I'm not wearing a stopwatch," Abby teased, slowing her pace to minimize the bumps.

When they reached the gate, Abby unhooked the latch and opened it, the rusty hinges squealing in protest. Then she pushed Mary through to the other side, but they still didn't see any sign of Finnegan.

"Where is he?" Mary's gaze scanned the dense woods. "Finnegan!"

The dog barked in reply, leading them further into the woods. Twigs snapped beneath the wheelchair as Abby pushed it along the flagstone path that led all the way down to the beach.

"I think I see him!" Mary pointed the way as Abby steered the wheelchair off the path and over a fragrant bed of pine needles.

They found the dog standing next to a large conifer, his nose almost touching a gray pigeon on the ground. It wasn't moving. The yellow tennis ball lay next to the pigeon.

"Finnegan," Mary called gently, holding out her hand to him.

He moved to her side and nuzzled her palm. "Good dog," she murmured softly, petting the top of his soft, furry head.

Abby bent down next to the pigeon, wondering how the bird had died. But to her surprise, she saw a tiny flutter in its delicate neck, then one eye opened to look up at her.

"It's alive," Abby told her sister.

Mary leaned forward for a better look. "What's wrong with it?"

Abby gently manipulated the bird's wing, careful not to startle it. "I think this wing is dislocated. And the poor thing looks like it's in a state of exhaustion."

She turned to her sister. "Can I use your apron?"

Mary didn't even hesitate. She pulled off her pink gingham apron, then handed it to Abby.

"Okay, let's do this nice and slow," Abby said, more to herself than to the pigeon.

Holding the apron in her hands to protect her fingers from the bird's sharp beak and claws, she tenderly lifted the pigeon off the ground. She placed one end of the apron completely over the bird to keep it calm as well as give it some extra warmth.

"Here," Mary said, reaching out her hands. "Let me hold it."

Abby settled the injured bird in Mary's lap, then they headed back toward the gate. Finnegan followed with the tennis ball in his mouth.

When they reached the house, Mary handed the pigeon to Abby once more, then reattached Finnegan's harness. Blossom opened her sleepy eyes and took one look at the commotion in the living room before leaping off the armchair and bounding out of the room.

"Are you going to take the pigeon to your lab at the conservatory?" Mary asked.

Abby hesitated, then shook her head. "Not tonight." Considering the bird's condition, she didn't want to move it any more than necessary. "Can I use one of your boxes to keep it in?"

"Of course," Mary replied, turning in the direction of her craft room to retrieve one of the deep cardboard boxes she used to store her dried flower arrangements.

Abby carried the bird into the kitchen, now toasty warm from the oven. A few moments later, Mary met her there and handed Abby the box. "Will this one do?"

"It's perfect. Thank you." Abby placed the bird inside. A quick glance told her it was a male. He was too weak to even attempt to escape. So weak in fact, that she wasn't sure the pigeon would survive the night.

"Is there anything else I can do?" Mary asked, Finnegan watching intently by her side.

Abby sighed. "There's really nothing either of us can do at this point. He's too weak to take any water or nourishment right now. I may try to give him something later this evening. His wing will eventually slip back into position on its own, though I may splint it. Hopefully, now that the pigeon is out of danger of predators and the elements, he'll recover."

Mary's gaze narrowed as she looked in the box. "What's that?"

"What?"

She pointed at the bird. "That yellow thing on his leg?"

Abby moved closer to the box, wondering what she'd

missed. Moving part of the apron aside, she saw a small, yellow tube tied to the pigeon's leg.

"He must be a homing pigeon," Abby said in amazement. "No wonder he's exhausted. He's probably been flying a long distance, maybe even hundreds of miles."

Homing pigeons had always fascinated her. Abby had read research papers speculating that the birds have a type of magnetic map inside their beak to help them navigate.

"A homing pigeon?" Mary echoed. "Does that mean he's carrying a message?"

"It certainly looks like it." Abby began untying the yellow tube, certain the bird would be more comfortable without it attached.

Abby pulled the tiny tube free and held it in her hand. This age-old method of communication stretched back for centuries. Now homing pigeons were bred more for racing than delivering messages, which made her even more intrigued about the tube in her hand.

"Should I open it?" Abby asked, torn between curiosity and a reluctance to invade someone's privacy.

Mary hesitated. "I suppose it is like opening somebody else's mail, but we might find a name or address of the owner of the pigeon. Who knows how long he's been gone or how worried his owner is at this moment."

Her sister had a point. If this was Abby's bird, she'd care much more about finding him than whether someone opened the tube and read the message inside.

Abby placed the gingham apron carefully back over the pigeon, who seemed to be resting more comfortably now inside the box. The fact that he wasn't spooked by human contact told her that someone had spent a lot of time with him.

"You're right," Abby agreed at last, breaking the seal on the tube. She removed the cap, then tipped the tube to one side. A tightly wrapped scroll of white paper slid into her palm. She unrolled it, smoothing the paper flat with her hand.

"What does it say?" Mary asked, leaning forward in her chair.

Abby stared at the message, baffled by what she saw there. It was series of letters and numbers printed by hand in bold, black ink.

"I don't know," she replied. "It doesn't make any sense." She held up the paper so Mary could see it. "I think it's in some form of code."

Mary rolled her wheelchair closer. "There's no name on it? No phone number?"

"Not that I can tell." Abby scanned the message again. "It all looks like gibberish to me."

"Well, it must mean something to somebody," Mary insisted. "Maybe we can decipher it."

"Maybe," Abby said, intrigued by the possibility. Then she turned back to the box, lifting the apron slightly to check on her patient.

"Where are you from?" she breathed, gently smoothing his feathers. "And where were you going?"

The pigeon cooed weakly, but his response was as much a mystery to Abby as the message he carried.

"Oh no," Mary cried, the panic in her tone bringing Finnegan to her side. "I forgot about the meatloaf!" She spun her wheelchair around and rolled over to the oven.

"Is it burned?" Abby asked.

Mary opened the oven door and poked at the meatloaf with a fork. "No, it's just a little crispy around the edges."

"I like it that way," Abby assured her. She turned her attention back to the homing pigeon. "I'll take him to the conservatory tomorrow along with the message. Maybe someone there can decipher it."

"We have to give him a name," Mary declared, grabbing two oven mitts and pulling them on before taking the meatloaf out. "We can't just keep calling him the pigeon."

"Do you have any suggestions?"

Mary set the meatloaf on the counter, letting it cool slightly before she cut into it. "Well, let's see . . . It's a boy, right?"

Abby nodded. "A fully grown *Columba livia*, which is a variety of domesticated rock dove. I wonder if he lost his way in that storm last night. The wind was really blowing hard."

"I bet he did." Mary set a basket of wheat rolls on the table.

"We could call him Windy," Abby suggested.

Mary laughed. "You've always been terrible with names. Remember when we were little and found that kitten in the barn? You wanted to call her Scratchy because she scratched you the first time you tried to pick her up."

"I was only seven," Abby said in her own defense.

"I think we should call him Homer," Mary said with a smile. "Since he's a homing pigeon. Besides, he looks like a Homer to me."

Abby had to admit she was right. "Okay, then. Homer it is."

Finnegan chuffed, signaling his approval.

"Dinner's ready," Mary announced, pulling a covered dish out of the refrigerator.

"Strawberry salad?" Abby said when she saw the bowl in her sister's lap. "That's one of my favorites!"

Mary grinned. "Dad dropped off some fresh strawberries from the farm today, so I thought I'd surprise you."

"Everything looks delicious," Abby said, her heart touched by Mary's thoughtfulness.

She placed a clean dish towel over the top of the box so Homer could rest. Then she joined her sister at the kitchen table.

As they said grace together, a familiar and comforting peace settled over Abby. Just like the missing baby orca and the homing pigeon, people sometimes strayed off course. She was glad her faith had always kept her paths straight.

Abby picked up her fork, then glanced at the box. If Homer recovered, it would be at least a week to two before he could fly long distances. That meant the message he was supposed to deliver would have to wait.

Abby just hoped it wasn't important.

CHAPTER ❦ THREE

THE NEXT MORNING, ABBY found a much perkier Homer in his box. She'd given him a little nourishment twice during the night, not wanting to over-burden his delicate system. When she walked into the kitchen to make herself a cup of hot tea, she heard him cooing from his corner.

"Good morning, Homer," she told the bird, pulling the dish towel off the top of the box. "Feeling better, are we?"

The pigeon blinked up at her. She could see Homer's wing still bothered him, so she didn't have to worry about his trying to fly out of his box. After steeping her tea, she took him out on the deck with her to enjoy some time in the sun.

With the box beside her, Abby settled into her chair for her morning devotional. She breathed in the fresh morning air, her gaze taking in the dewy brilliance of the day. Then she opened the Bible in her lap to the Book of Matthew.

"Ask and it will be given you," she read softly to herself, "seek and you will find; knock and the door will be opened to you.

For everyone who asks receives; he who seeks finds; and to him who knocks, the door will be opened" (Matthew 7:7–8).

The Scripture reminded Abby of the power of prayer. She closed her eyes, praying for God's guidance and for the strength to accomplish the tasks set before her. When she finished her devotional, a calm resolve settled over her and she couldn't wait to start her day.

She carried Homer's box back into the kitchen, where she found Mary already making breakfast. Her sister looked up as Abby walked through the door, greeting her with a smile.

"How about some blueberry pancakes to start off the weekend?" Mary offered, stirring the bowl of batter in her lap.

"That sounds wonderful." Abby set Homer's box on the counter and rinsed her empty tea cup in the sink. "I have a lot to do today, so I'll have to make it a quick breakfast."

"They'll be ready in a jiffy," Mary promised, pouring circles of batter onto the hot griddle. Then she wheeled over to take a peek in Homer's box. "He looks better today."

The pigeon cooed in affirmation.

"Yes, he's much better," Abby wiped her wet hands on a dish towel. "I need to get him settled in at the lab, then I'm off to interview some of the whale-watch tour boat captains. Hopefully, they'll be able to tell me something about how that mother orca was injured Thursday night."

Mary returned to the griddle to flip the pancakes. "I hope her missing orca calf is found soon."

"So do I."

Thirty minutes later, Abby arrived at the conservatory with Homer in tow. She went straight to the laboratory, where she often brought injured birds and wildlife. After putting on her lab coat, she checked the microcassette recorder she kept in the pocket to make certain it had enough tape left.

It was a recent purchase, and she found it much easier to record her notes while she was working with birds in the lab or out in the field rather than jotting them down on paper. The recorder was voice-activated, so she didn't have to turn it on and off. It simply started recording at the sound of a human voice.

Abby attached a small splint to Homer's injured wing then transferred him from his box to a nice clean cage. Because the pigeon was so tame, unlike most of the wild birds in the lab, Abby stayed with him for a while until he got acclimated to his new environment. She watched Homer check out his new home and was relieved to see him take a few sips of water.

The door to the laboratory opened, and Abby turned around to see Bobby McDonald race inside. One of the wild ducks that she'd been rehabilitating quacked at his sudden appearance.

"Wait until you see what I've got!" he said, his hazel eyes dancing with excitement.

Abby smiled at his exuberance. The ten-year-old radiated an energy and joy that made her relish spending time with him. The McDonalds lived next door to Abby and Mary. Bobby often helped out around the house and yard.

"Wait until you see what *I've* got," Abby replied. "But you go first."

Bobby pulled a small silver camera out of his backpack and held it out to her. "Isn't it cool! I've been saving my money for a really long time and finally bought it yesterday."

"It's very nice," Abby said, "but don't you already have a camera?"

"Yes, but this one's digital," he said proudly, "just like yours."

Bobby had long admired the digital camera that Abby carried in her birding vest. He especially liked the fact that it didn't use film, but recorded pictures on a memory card that could then be loaded onto a computer.

Abby found herself taking many more pictures with her digital camera than she had with her 35mm camera. The pictures that didn't turn out well she could easily delete, saving money in the long run on film and developing.

"It's a used camera," he explained, "but in really good condition."

Abby knew the McDonalds couldn't afford many extravagances and was impressed that a boy Bobby's age could be so thrifty with his money. "That sounds like a smart buy."

His smile widened. "I've been taking lots of pictures. Do you want to see some of them?"

"Sure." Abby looked over his shoulder at the small display screen on the back of his camera. Bobby pressed a button and pictures began to slowly flash past her on the screen.

"Here are some of my mom and dad," Bobby explained. "We went on a picnic at Lopez Island yesterday to celebrate the start of summer vacation."

"These are great," Abby said, noting that Bobby had taken many scenic beach shots as well as some with people and wildlife.

"There are a lot more," he said, putting the camera down. "But you said you had something to show me." He looked around the lab. "Is it a new bird?"

"It sure is." Abby led him to Homer's cage. "Finnegan found him yesterday in the back yard. He's a homing pigeon, so we named him Homer."

Bobby bent down until he was eye-level with the bird. "Hello, Homer."

Homer cooed at him, flapping his good wing as he walked back and forth in his cage.

"I think he likes me," Bobby said, then turned to Abby. "Is he sick or something?"

"Just very tired and recovering from a dislocated wing. Homing pigeons can travel hundreds of miles. I don't know how far he'd flown when we found him."

"He does look kind of skinny," Bobby observed.

"Will you take his picture for me?" Abby asked. "Then we can compare it to how Homer looks after we fatten him up. He's going to need to regain some weight and some strength before we let him travel again."

Bobby took careful aim with his camera. "Smile, Homer."

The bird cooed at him again as Bobby snapped the picture.

Abby looked over his shoulder as the picture appeared on the display screen. "That's a great shot, Bobby."

"I can make it any size you want once I put it on the computer. I can even put Homer's name on it."

"That's a good idea. Then we can tape the picture onto the wall above his cage." Abby ruffled the dark brown hair on the boy's head, making his cowlick stand up even more. "You're turning into quite a photographer."

"Thanks," he said, a proud blush on his cheeks. "I've been reading some photography books from the library. All about how to use lighting and perspective."

Bobby's thirst for knowledge knew no bounds. His keen intellect had challenged her on more than one occasion, and Abby sensed that he had a bright future ahead of him.

A knock sounded on the door to the laboratory, and Mick

Wymore stuck his blond head inside. "I hope I'm not interrupting your work. Hugo told me I could find you here."

Abby couldn't judge from Mick's expression whether he had good news or bad news about the missing orca calf. She hoped Poppy had been found alive and returned to the K pod, although she still intended to conduct her investigation no matter what.

"Please come in." Abby placed one hand on Bobby's narrow shoulder. "I'd like you to meet a good friend of mine. His name is Bobby McDonald. Bobby, this is Mick Wymore. He's a marine biologist."

"Wow, for real?"

Mick laughed. "For real." He reached out to shake the boy's hand. "Nice to meet you, Bobby. That's quite a camera you've got there."

"Thanks, I just bought it." Bobby grinned up at him. "It's digital."

"Very cool," Mick affirmed. "I actually used an underwater digital camera when I was preparing my master's thesis."

Bobby's eyes widened. "An underwater camera? That would be so awesome!"

Mick nodded. "I'll have to remember to bring it ashore the next time I come to Sparrow Island so you can try it out."

Abby watched the interaction between the two of them, impressed by Mick's ability to connect with Bobby so easily. The man had a natural charm and a sunny disposition that made him easy to like.

"Can I take your picture?" Bobby asked, holding up his camera.

"Sure." Mick moved next to Abby. "How about if you take a picture of both of us?"

Abby didn't consider herself very photogenic, unlike Mary, who had never taken a bad picture in her life. "I don't need to be in the picture."

"Sure you do," Mick insisted, draping one arm loosely around her shoulder. "Then I can send a copy to Dr. Sima at Cornell to prove I really did meet you."

"Come on, Abby," Bobby entreated. "Just one picture. Please?"

Abby laughed, knowing she didn't stand a chance with these two charmers egging her on. "Okay, but you have to promise to delete any that don't turn out well."

"I promise." Bobby said. The boy stepped back a few feet from them to get a better angle. He took aim through the viewfinder, then frowned, putting the camera down to give them direction.

"Let's move a little closer to the window. We'll get a much better contrast of light and shadow there."

Abby suppressed a smile at the professional tone in his voice. She and Mick moved toward the window where Bobby placed them in position.

"Okay," he announced, aiming his camera at them once more. "Say . . . cheeseburgers."

"Cheeseburgers," Mick and Abby chorused in unison, the word provoking a grin from both of them.

The camera flashed, then Bobby looked at the display screen to view the result. "Oops, it looks like Abby has her eyes closed. We'd better take another one."

Abby and Mick stood together again as Bobby prepared to take another picture. "Okay, this time let's say . . . snickerdoodles."

"Snickerdoodles," Abby and Mick echoed together.

She knew that snickerdoodles were one of Bobby's favorite cookies and made a mental note to make him a batch soon.

"This one turned out great." Bobby held out the camera so Mick and Abby could take a look. "Are there any other pictures you want me to take?"

"Not right now," Mick replied, "but I definitely want a copy of that one."

Abby couldn't wait any longer for information about the missing orca calf. She turned to Mick. "Did you have any luck in your search for Poppy yesterday?"

Mick sighed and shook his head. "I'm afraid not. I conducted a perimeter search from the point of the K pod disturbance but didn't see any sign of Poppy."

Bobby crinkled his brow in confusion. "Who's Poppy?"

"An orca calf who's missing from the K pod," Mick replied.

"A boat apparently sailed through K pod Thursday night," Abby explained, "and injured a mother orca named Rosie. Now her baby, who's about six months old, is missing."

Bobby's mouth dropped open. "A baby orca? I think I saw it!"

Mick and Abby exchanged shocked glances. If it was true, Abby knew it meant Poppy was still alive. But she didn't want to get her hopes up.

"Where did you see it, Bobby?"

"By Lopez Island, when I was taking pictures there on our picnic yesterday. I thought it was a big dolphin at first, but it wasn't the right color. And it looked too small to be a whale."

Mick clapped him on the back. "Kid, you'll be a hero if you still have that picture."

"I think I do." Bobby began flipping through the pictures on the display screen on the back of his camera. "I hope I didn't delete it."

Abby hoped so too. She and Mick stood behind Bobby, watching as picture after picture flashed by on the small screen.

"Here it is!" Bobby exclaimed.

Mick leaned closer. "The picture's so small, I can't tell if that's an orca calf in the water or not."

"We could enlarge it on the computer," Bobby suggested. "All I have to do is download the pictures, and we can make the picture as big as we want."

Abby started toward the door, anticipation quickening her step. "I've already got the digital camera software on my laptop, so it's ready to go."

Mick and Bobby followed Abby to her office in The Nature Museum, where she let Bobby sit at her desk and download the pictures from the camera into her laptop computer.

A few minutes later, the picture Bobby took of the mysterious creature in the water started to appear on the computer screen.

"There it is," Bobby said, pointing to a lone dorsal fin protruding from the water. But it was too far away to tell if it was a dolphin or the missing orca calf.

"Can you enlarge it?" Abby asked.

"Easy," Bobby replied, clicking a few buttons on the keyboard. After a few moments, another picture loaded onto the screen.

Abby's breath caught in her throat as the picture became clear. "That has to be Poppy."

"The missing orca calf," Mick confirmed. "Alone in the sound."

Abby could see why Bobby might have mistaken it for a large dolphin from a distance, but the enlarged photograph revealed the unmistakable black and white markings of an orca.

Relief flowed through her. "At least we know Poppy's still alive."

"She's probably just lost and doesn't know how to find her way back home." Mick turned to Bobby. "Do you remember exactly where you took this picture?"

The boy hesitated. "I think it was on the north side of Lopez Island. Do you want me to print the picture out for you?"

"That would help," Mick replied. "I'm going to go out this morning and conduct another search in that area. If we're lucky, Poppy will still be there."

Abby turned on the printer while Bobby used some of the software tools on the computer to make the picture even sharper. Then she reached down to give the boy a hug. "Thank you, Bobby. This was just the clue we needed."

Bobby grinned up at her. "I knew my digital camera would come in handy."

Abby hoped it would lead them to the missing orca calf. As with other search-and-rescue missions she had been involved in, she recognized the same emotions flowing through her now. The worry. The hope. The fear of running out of time.

Mick obviously sensed it, too, because he kept shifting from one foot to the other, anxiously waiting for the picture to print.

After what seemed like an eternity, the picture of the orca calf emerged from the printer. "Here you go," Bobby said, handing it to him.

"Thank you." Mick studied the picture. "Poppy doesn't look like she's injured. At least, I don't see any visible wounds."

"We'll just have to hope for the best," Abby told him. "The sooner we locate Poppy, the sooner we can help her."

Mick nodded, then headed toward the door. "I'll let you know what I find." Then he hesitated, turning to face her in the doorway. "Unless you want to come with me?"

Abby was very tempted by his offer, but she had her own search to conduct. "Thank you, Mick, but I'm going over to Friday Harbor to talk to the whale-watch tour boat operators. I'm hoping one of them might be able to tell me how the K pod was disturbed."

"Sounds good." He gave them a brisk wave and was out the door.

Abby could hear his footsteps practically running down the hallway. She admired his enthusiasm. It made her all the more anxious to start her own search.

Bobby looked up at her. "I don't understand. Why would anyone want to hurt a mother orca and her baby?"

"I don't know," she replied, trying not to think the worst. "Maybe they didn't mean to do it. Or they got scared after their boat collided with the mother orca and didn't stick around long enough to see if she was hurt."

"But how could they not care?" Bobby said, truly puzzled by the callousness of such an act.

Abby wished she knew the answer, but she was just as bewildered. That's why she couldn't just let it go without discovering who was responsible.

And why she had to make sure it never happened again.

Huntington City Township
Public Library
200 West Market Street
Huntington, IN 46750

CHAPTER ❦ FOUR

Abby reached the quaint seaport of Friday Harbor on San Juan Island shortly before noon. A busy place on a Saturday, the marina allowed easy access to the parks, restaurants and shops on the island.

As she disembarked from the ferry, Abby saw the booking office of one of the whale-watch tour boats, *The Luna*, directly across the street, so she decided to head there first.

But to her surprise the office was closed. According to the schedule posted in the window, *The Luna* launched every weekday at two o'clock in the afternoon for a four-hour tour and twice on the weekends.

"That's strange," she murmured.

The Luna was one of the oldest and most respected lines in the whale-watch tour boat business. The owners were Seth and Margie Anderson, a husband and wife team who were good friends with Abby's parents. Seth was the captain and Margie a certified naturalist who did most of the narration on the tour.

Abby had briefly met the couple a few months ago when she'd stopped by Stanton Farm during an errand run. They had seemed like nice people, though she'd only spoken to them for a few minutes.

Since they were already acquainted, Abby wanted to interview them first, hoping they might have some valuable information about the orca incident. But with the office closed and no signs of life aboard *The Luna*, Abby wasn't sure what to do next.

Her stomach growled, giving her a clue. It was time for lunch. The savory aroma of roasting meat and onions led her to a portable cart called Barney's Gourmet Hot Dogs.

Barney Magee had been a fixture at the Friday Harbor marina for as long as she could remember. Even as a little girl, when she'd sailed with her father on his charter boat, they'd always stopped for one of Barney's delicious hot dogs.

Now, as she waited her turn in a line of tourists, Abby could see that Barney had aged considerably over the last thirty-five years. He wore a long-sleeved, blue-and-white-striped flannel shirt and navy blue trousers. A long white apron covered both.

He moved slowly, his shoulders bent with age. Sparse strands of snow white hair were combed over the top of his smooth pate. Thin, arthritic fingers cradled the hot dog buns as he filled each order.

But he still handled those hotdogs like an expert, slathering on the ketchup, mustard and relish with a flair that made her mouth water.

Despite the long wait, Abby knew one of Barney's hot dogs was worth it. When she reached the stainless steel cart, she smiled at the older man, certain she'd changed even more than he had in the intervening years. She was no longer the young girl in pigtails who used to stand on her tip-toes to place an order.

"May I help you, miss?" Barney asked, a twinkle in his blue eyes.

"I'll have a footlong, please. And a glass of iced tea."

He reached for a bun. "Would you like the works on that footlong?"

"Yes, I would. With some extra relish and mustard, please."

He smiled up at her. "That like a woman who knows what she wants. Where do you hail from?"

"Actually, I live on Sparrow Island. I'm Abby Stanton."

"Abby Stanton," he murmured to himself, then looked at her in surprise. "Stanton . . . not George Stanton's little girl?"

"One and the same," Abby replied with a smile, pleased that he'd remembered her.

"Well, I'll be," he said, his face shining with delight. "I remember way back when you used to come by my stand with your dad. You were such a little squirt, but you sure could put away a hot dog."

She laughed. "I still can, though it's been a while."

"Well let's see if you're still an expert," he said as he handed her the foil-wrapped footlong. "Today's dog is on me. I hope you enjoy it."

"Thank you," she said, taking the hot dog from him.

He set her iced tea on the counter between them, then picked up his tongs and rotated the hot dogs on his roaster. "So what are you doing now, Abby?"

"I'm an ornithologist. I work at the Sparrow Island Nature Conservatory."

Barney set down the tongs and leaned against the counter, relaxing now that there was a lull in customers. "Imagine that."

"I love my work," she told him, peeling back the foil from her footlong.

"George must be very proud of you," Barney said.

"I hope so," Abby mused.

"Looks like you're enjoying that hot dog," he teased. "There's nothing better than a one-of-a-kind, slow-roasted Barney's gourmet hot dog."

She laughed, then took a bite of her footlong. It was strange how a familiar taste or smell could bring back memories of her childhood. She'd spent so many happy hours with her father aboard his boat that just the taste of a Barney's hot dog on her tongue brought it all rushing back to her.

"So was it my hot dogs that brought you to Friday Harbor today or something else?"

She licked a dollop of ketchup off her thumb. "Actually, I was hoping to talk with Seth and Margie Anderson, but they don't seem to be around. The booking office for *The Luna* is closed."

"Seth and Margie?" Barney hitched a thumb toward the town. "Oh, they're over at the insurance office, turning in a claim." He shook his head with a forlorn sigh. "I don't know when they'll be open for business again. If ever."

"A claim?" Abby echoed. "What happened?"

"A terrible thing," he replied. "I haven't seen anything like it in all my years here. You probably didn't notice it when you got off the ferry, but one side of *The Luna* is all banged up. If you go further down the dock, you can see the damage."

"How did that happen?"

He gave a small shrug. "Vandalism is what I heard. There's too much damage to risk taking *The Luna* out on the water, that's for sure."

Damage from hitting the mother orca?

Abby didn't even want to consider that possibility, but she couldn't deny the thought had entered her mind.

"Come on, I'll show you," Barney said, placing a BE BACK SOON sign on the top of his hot dog cart.

"Oh, I don't want to take you away from your business."

"It's time for a break anyway," he assured her. "I need to stretch these old legs of mine from time to time. Otherwise they stiffen up on me something terrible."

As Abby followed him down the street toward *The Luna*, she guessed his age to be almost eighty. She wondered if she'd still be going as strong at that age, maybe even still leading birding tours and working at the conservatory.

Barney, her parents and Iona Benson were all wonderful examples of people who didn't let their age stop them from enjoying life to the fullest. If God continued to bless her with good health, Abby planned to do the same.

When they reached the dock where *The Luna* was moored, Barney took her around to the port side and showed her the damage.

Abby stared at the boat in disbelief. A large dent near the waterline had crumpled the steel hull. "When did this happen?"

"They discovered it yesterday morning when they came to open the booking office for the day," Barney replied. "They filed a police report right away. Once they saw the extent of the damage, they had to cancel all of their scheduled tours. It's not safe go out on the water until they make sure the integrity of the hull isn't compromised."

Abby knelt down on the dock to get a closer look at the damage. It had to have been something large and heavy that caused a dent of that size. An orca, perhaps?

The mother orca had been injured some time Thursday night. That meant the timing was right. But for what possible reason would the Andersons sail through the K pod?

She didn't want to believe it. Seth and Margie Anderson had impressed her as good, honest folks—people who cared about the environment.

But the coincidence seemed too overwhelming.

"Nobody knows how it happened?" Abby asked. "No witnesses?"

Barney shook his head. "Nobody seems to have a clue. Strange, isn't it?"

"It certainly is." Perhaps the Andersons had hit the mother orca unknowingly, though Abby knew it would be hard to miss the jolt such a collision would produce. Besides, they'd been in the business long enough to know how to avoid getting too close to the orca pods.

Unless they did it intentionally to collect the insurance money.

Abby hated to even think of that possibility, although she couldn't deny that the Andersons were getting older, certainly past the age when most people started thinking about retirement.

But why not just sell the boat? Surely that would make more sense than sailing through an orca pod with the intention of hitting a nine-ton whale.

"Did *The Luna* go out on any tours on Thursday?" she asked.

"Two that I know of," Barney said. "The regular afternoon tour, then a private charter on Thursday evening. I closed up my hot dog cart and left for home before they came back."

She doubted the incident could have happened during the afternoon tour. Even tourists on their first whale-watch expedition would have noticed sailing through an orca pod—especially if they had collided with one of the orcas.

If the Andersons had hit the mother orca, it would have

been during the private tour. Or later, if the Andersons—or someone else—had taken *The Luna* out for a solo ride.

"Does anyone besides Seth ever captain the boat?" Abby asked Barney.

He shook his head. "Nope. He doesn't let anyone but him or Margie ever take over the controls of *The Luna*. It's their baby."

Abby nodded. It all seemed to add up: the injured mother orca; the dent in the hull of *The Luna*; the Andersons collecting insurance money for the damage. Simple.

Maybe too simple.

The clues were there, but Abby sensed she was missing something important. She needed to talk to the Andersons and hear their side of the story.

ABBY LINGERED AT THE DOCK for over an hour, perusing the kiosks set up to attract tourists. She even bought a small brooch exquisitely carved out of tupelo wood in the shape of a bird. It reminded her of Homer and the price made it impossible to resist. At last, she saw the Andersons arrive at the marina and head toward *The Luna*.

They were dressed in identical black warm-up suits adorned with white piping and had the same short gray hair and green eyes. The couple looked even more alike than they had the first time she'd met them.

"Hello," she called out, hurrying to intercept them before they could board their damaged boat.

Margie turned toward her. "Well, hello, Abby. How nice to see you again." She looked up at her husband. "Seth, you remember Abby Stanton, George and Ellen's younger daughter?"

He reached out to shake her hand. "Of course. How are you, Abby?"

"I'm fine," she said, feeling even more certain now that this pleasant couple couldn't be responsible for injuring Rosie. But she had to follow every lead.

"What brings you to Friday Harbor today?" Margie asked.

She needed to tread carefully and not accuse them outright since that could potentially ruin their friendship with her parents.

"I just ate one of Barney's wonderful hot dogs. I haven't had one in over thirty-five years."

They both smiled, the sadness in their eyes shadowing their amusement.

"Barney is one-of-a-kind," Seth said wistfully. "We enjoy seeing him every day when we come to work. His hot dogs are definitely worth the trip from Sparrow Island."

Abby nodded. "Barney told me about the damage to *The Luna*. That must have been a terrible shock for you."

Seth looked grim. "It was, Abby. I still can't believe it."

"Do you have any idea how it might have happened?" Abby asked gently.

Margie shook her head. "We don't have a clue. Everything was fine when we docked the boat here Thursday night. We were out late, just past midnight, but we certainly would have heard—and felt—a collision with something that caused that much damage to our boat."

Abby's instincts told her they were telling the truth. "Barney said you took the boat out on a private tour."

Seth nodded. "A couple from Phoenix was here celebrating their twenty-fifth wedding anniversary. They wanted a moon-light tour."

Abby thought about that for a moment. "But wasn't it hard for them to see anything in the dark?"

Seth chuckled. "They were more interested in looking at each other."

"It was so sweet," Margie said. "They just wanted the boat all to themselves so they could sail under the stars and hold hands."

"So they weren't interested in seeing any orcas?" Abby asked.

Seth and Margie exchanged glances.

"We know what people are saying," Margie said, her voice tight. "That we sailed through the K pod and damaged the hull by hitting the mother orca. But I can assure you that didn't happen."

"I never said—" Abby began.

But Seth interrupted her, clearly upset with the rumors apparently flying about them. "We're members of the Whale Watch Operators Association Northwest. That's a group of tour boat companies dedicated to the responsible viewing of wildlife."

"We've been members for twenty years," Margie cut in. "The association sets safety guidelines for operating vessels around the orcas and other wildlife. We've always followed those guidelines to the letter."

Their fervent defense convinced Abby as much as her intuition that the Andersons weren't responsible for injuring Rosie.

"I believe someone is trying to frame us," Seth said, his shoulders wilting. "That's the only reason I can think of for the damage to our boat."

That reasoning made the most sense to Abby too. "But why would anyone do such a thing?"

Margie sighed, then glanced up at her husband. "That's what we've been asking ourselves since yesterday. And we can only come up with one conclusion. Someone's trying to put us out of business."

Abby looked between the two of them. "Another tour boat operator?"

Seth nodded. "That's the most obvious explanation. When we left here Thursday night, *The Luna* was fine. On Friday morning," he pointed to the damaged hull, "we found her like this."

"Do you have any suspects?" Abby asked.

"There are four whale-watching tour boats, including ours, that run the K pod route out of Friday Harbor," Margie replied. "*The Polaris, The Adventurer* and *The Sea Prince.* The competition for passengers can be fierce."

No doubt *The Luna's* longevity in the business and the respect the Andersons had garnered over the years made the other tour boat captains envy them. But enough to try to destroy their success?

"We don't have any proof," Margie said, as if reading Abby's mind. "Just speculation at this point. To be honest with you, Abby, I don't even want it to be true. I can't imagine anyone purposefully hurting an orca just to damage our boat and our reputation."

Abby couldn't imagine it, either. But someone had sailed through the orca pod and injured Rosie. Someone had caused enough disruption to the K pod to separate Poppy from her family. Now she was missing and Abby was determined to unravel this ocean mystery.

"Thank you for telling me all of this," Abby said. "I know it must be difficult for you."

Seth reached for his wife's hand. "We've been through worse together. And with God's help, we'll get through this too."

Abby watched them board the crippled *Luna*, convinced in her heart that they were innocent. Now she was even more determined to find the culprit so she could clear their name. The Andersons didn't deserve to have their business—and their lives—ruined by even a shadow of suspicion.

CHAPTER ❀ FIVE

"Fumet," SGT. HENRY COBB said aloud as he placed the tiles on the Scrabble board. "That's a triple word score for me."

Abby sat with Mary and her beau at the dining room table, enjoying a friendly game after dinner. The rays of the setting sun shone through the windows, casting a golden glow about the room.

She relished the opportunity to relax after spending most of her Saturday trying to track down the captains of the other tour boats. All three of them had been out on whale-watching expeditions, so she'd left messages with their booking agents, asking them to contact her as soon as possible.

Mary was winning the game with Abby a close second. Poor Henry was so far behind that neither one of them wanted to challenge him on the strange word he'd just placed on the board.

"Well?" he asked, arching a brow in Mary's direction. The couple enjoyed competing with each other, though Abby's sister usually came out on top.

"*Fumet*," Mary said. "That's a different word. I don't think I've ever heard it before. How about you, Abby?"

She shook her head. "No, I don't think so. Sorry, Henry."

"Not as strange as *xylem*," Henry countered, pointing to the word that Mary had placed on the Scrabble board during an earlier turn.

"*Xylem* is a type of tissue in plants," Mary explained with a wide smile. "You lost the challenge, Henry, and lost your turn in the process, remember?"

Henry sighed. "How am I supposed to compete with a florist and an ornithologist? You two know so many fancy scientific words it makes my head spin. It's like you're speaking in code."

Mary looked at Abby. "Speaking of codes, why don't we let Henry take a crack at deciphering that message we found on Homer."

"Good idea," Abby said, rising from her chair to retrieve the note. After fishing it out of her bag, she walked over to the table and handed it to Henry.

"What's this?" he asked, studying the paper in front of him. "A puzzle or something?"

"We think it's some kind of code," Mary replied, "but we can't figure it out. We found the note on an injured homing pigeon that Finnegan discovered in the woods last night."

"Interesting," Henry studied the code, his brow furrowed. "Three separate lines of letters and numbers with no breaks in between them. Do you have any idea where the homing pigeon came from?"

"None," Abby replied. "Homing pigeons have been known to travel several hundred miles. Poor Homer was exhausted when we found him."

"Homer?" Henry interjected, looking between the two women.

"That's his name," Mary explained. "He's so cute and he looks like a Homer."

Henry laughed. "A homing pigeon named Homer. Well, that certainly fits. So how far did Homer travel?"

"There's really no way to tell," Abby replied. "He'd lost a lot of conditioning on the flight, so I'm guessing it was quite a distance."

Henry turned his attention back to the note. "Police use codes. Both letters and numbers to identify different crimes in progress or as a kind of short-hand to ask for help. But the codes I know look nothing like this one."

Abby tried to hide her disappointment. She'd been hoping Henry would know how to crack the code. The longer the coded message remained a mystery, the more curious she became.

"I've never seen anything like it, either," Abby said. "I'm worried that the note might contain something important and that Homer won't arrive with the message soon enough."

"It could just be some kids playing around," Mary ventured. "I can't imagine any reason why adults would use a secret code to communicate instead of simply picking up the telephone."

"Unless it involves something criminal," Henry suggested. "I remember reading a book about the Prohibition Era, when rum runners would use secret codes to communicate with their partners on shore."

Abby hadn't even considered that possibility. Whoever had written that note wanted to hide something. She just didn't know what or why.

"Maybe Homer's carrying messages for smugglers," Mary guessed. "Or plans for a robbery or some other crime."

"Maybe." Abby sighed. "We'll never know unless we decipher the code."

Henry finally gave up, handing the note back to Abby. "Well, I'm sorry to say that I don't have a clue. Now, are you two just trying to distract me from the game while I'm making my big comeback?"

Mary laughed. "We're still waiting for you to tell us what *fumet* means."

"It means a pleasant aroma," Henry informed them. "Like that pleasant aroma of apple pie that hit me as soon as I walked into the house tonight. I think I'll have another slice after I win this game."

Mary arched a brow in her sister's direction. "What do you think, Abby? Shall we let him have the points for *fumet* or do we want to challenge?"

The doorbell rang before Abby could answer. "I think I'll go answer the door while you two work this out."

She rose out of her chair and headed for the living room. The doorbell rang again before she could reach the door.

"I'm coming," she murmured, wondering about the identity of the impatient person on the other side of the door.

She opened it to find a stranger standing on the front step. He was a tall, slender man with short dark hair that curled around the edges of the black knit hat he wore on his head. That, along with the black pea coat he wore, reminded her of a sailor.

"Hello," she said. She might have been more apprehensive if Henry wasn't sitting at the dining room table.

"I'm looking for Dr. Stanton," he said, his voice low and gruff. "Seth Anderson told me I could find her here."

"I'm Dr. Stanton," she replied, suppressing a shiver at the cool breeze drifting in from outside.

"My name is Lewis Hovel," he said stiffly. "I got a message that you were looking for me today."

Abby blinked, surprised to find the captain of *The Adventurer* standing at her door. He looked older than her fifty-five years, but she knew a life on the sea could weather a man. His face was deeply lined, though he was still quite handsome.

She opened the door wider. "Please come in, Captain Hovel."

He walked inside and removed his hat. "I know it's rather late, Dr. Stanton, but I wanted to get this matter settled right away and I thought it was important to do it face-to-face."

His terse tone told Abby that she'd offended him in some way. "Please, call me Abby. I assume you got my message."

His jaw twitched. "Indeed, I did. And I must tell you that I do not appreciate the accusation that *The Adventurer* is responsible for disrupting that orca pod."

Henry appeared in the doorway between the living room and the foyer. "Is there a problem, Abby?" he asked, concern resonating in his voice.

"No," Abby assured him. "Everything's fine."

Henry hesitated for a moment, his gaze sizing up Hovel, then he returned to the dining room.

Abby turned back to Captain Hovel. "I didn't accuse you of disrupting the K pod," she said calmly. "I simply told your booking agent that I was looking into the incident and was hoping you might have some information to help me discover what happened."

"That's not what she told me," Captain Hovel said, then his expression softened. "Then again, Rhonda isn't the best listener. Perhaps she misunderstood you."

Relieved to have cleared up the confusion, Abby motioned him toward the living room. "Please, sit down, Captain Hovel.

May I offer you something? A cup of coffee, perhaps? We have apple pie too."

He walked over to the sofa. "Coffee sounds wonderful. I just ate dinner or I'd take you up on that pie."

"Please make yourself comfortable," Abby told him as she headed for the kitchen. "I'll be right back."

When Abby passed through the dining room, she found both Mary and Henry looking curiously at her.

"Who was at the door?" Mary asked. "I thought I heard a man's voice."

"It's Lewis Hovel," Abby replied softly so her guest wouldn't overhear. "He's the captain of *The Adventurer*, one of the whale-watch tour boats on San Juan Island. The message I left with his booking agent seems to have ruffled a few of his feathers."

They followed her into the kitchen. "Or maybe it's the sign of a guilty conscience," Mary suggested.

"Would you like me to have a word with him?" Henry asked Abby. "I didn't hear exactly what he said, but I didn't like the man's tone."

"Oh no," Abby assured him, pouring two cups of coffee. "We cleared up the confusion, and I invited him to stay for a cup of coffee. This is a good chance for me to talk to him about the injured mother orca. So you two go ahead and finish the game without me. I'm not sure how long this will take."

"Don't worry," Mary assured her. "We'll wait for you."

Abby left the two of them together and returned to the living room. She handed Captain Hovel his cup. "I forgot to ask if you take cream or sugar."

"Neither, thank you. I like my coffee hot, strong and black." He took a cautious sip, then smiled up at her. "This is just right."

Abby sat down across from him. "I don't believe we've ever met before, Captain Hovel. How long have you lived on the islands?"

"Just about a year now," he replied, leaning back against the sofa. "I've always been a wanderer, but the San Juan Islands seem like home to me. I don't think I'll ever want to leave."

Abby felt the same way. Now that she'd reconnected with her home and her family, she couldn't imagine living anywhere else. There were times she missed her friends and colleagues at Cornell, as well as the students she'd taught there. But those happy memories only enhanced her life here on Sparrow Island and she looked forward to making new memories.

She wondered about Captain Hovel's background and why he didn't have any place to call home. "Where else have you lived, Captain?"

He cradled his coffee cup in his large, weather-worn hands. "Well, let's see now . . . I started off in the merchant marines and spent most of my time traveling in the Pacific. I've lived in Japan, the Philippines, Guam, but I never really did settle down anywhere."

"So how did you get started in the whale-watch tour boat business?" Abby asked him, genuinely interested.

"A friend of mine had a charter boat in Maine—a forty-six-foot, twin-engine beauty. He hired me on as part of his crew for whale-watching tours. When he decided to sell the business, I'd saved up enough money to buy the boat from him. I stayed in Maine for a while, but the weather's a bit too cold there for me."

Abby could appreciate his desire for a change of scenery and climate. "So that's when you decided to head for the Pacific Northwest?"

He nodded. "I'd heard great things about this part of the world and decided to take a look for myself. Can't say I'm disappointed."

Abby sipped her coffee, somewhat surprised he was this open about his life after that tense meeting at the front door. She knew better then to judge people by first impressions and Captain Hovel seemed like a man who needed time to warm up to strangers, which made her wonder about his interaction with his passengers.

Then again, he might leave that to his crew and restrict himself to running the boat.

"How long have you been in the charter boat business?" she asked him.

He cocked one eyebrow toward the ceiling, thinking over her question. "Must be about fifteen years now."

"So you must enjoy meeting new people."

Captain Hovel gave her a sheepish smile. "I'm a good enough businessman to know that I'm not a people-person. So I just navigate the boat and let one of my crew do all the talking."

That confirmed her instincts about the man and she admired the fact that he could be honest about it. Would he be as honest about what he knew regarding the incident with the K pod?

She hesitated, still remembering his reaction when she'd first opened the door. Maybe Mary was right and he did suffer from a guilty conscience. Or perhaps, like the Andersons, he didn't want to be falsely accused of a crime he hadn't commited.

"I have to admit," he said, filling the silence, "that it's been a little tough for me to get to know people here. Of course, I spend most of my time on *The Adventurer,* so it's not like it's handy for people to stop by and visit me."

"If you'd like to meet new people, you're always welcome to come join us at the Little Flock Church on Sunday morning," Abby told him. "Services start at ten o'clock. It's a wonderful way to meet new people, and I know everyone would be glad to have you there."

"Thanks for the invitation," he replied, without indicating if he intended to take her up on it.

"Have you had a chance to join the Whale Watch Operators Association Northwest?" she asked. "I'm sure you could find people there who share your interests."

He grimaced. "I have to admit that I'm not much of a joiner. I'm of the opinion that a man should do the right thing whether or not he's a member of some do-good organization."

Abby agreed, though she believed that when people came together in a common cause, they could do great and wonderful things. Her church was proof of that. The faith the congregation members shared empowered them to have a positive impact on their community and beyond.

"I'll be honest," he continued, "having one of those Whale Watch Operators Association Northwest stickers on the office window probably would bring in more business. Guess I'll have to join up one of these days."

She watched him and wondered how many questions she could ask before he took offense. Yet, the only way to discover who sailed through the orca pod would be to interview those in the business.

"So how did you hear the news about the injured orca?" she asked at last.

"I saw the whale myself," he replied, "after she beached herself on Lopez Island." He shook his head. "I've seen beached whales before and it's a sad, sad sight. Most of them don't make it, you know."

Abby nodded, grateful that Rosie was an exception to this rule. Her baby was still lost, however, and that fact made it difficult for Abby to sleep at night.

"So are you a cop or something?" Captain Hovel asked, doing a little prying of his own. "Because you sure do ask a lot of questions."

She laughed. "Not even close." Abby wasn't sure if she should tell him there was a cop sitting in the next room. "I'm an ornithologist."

"A what?"

"A bird specialist. I work at the Sparrow Island Nature Conservatory."

"Oh," he said, confusion etched on his face. "So if you're into birds, why are you asking around about who hit that orca?"

"I don't like to see any wildlife injured," Abby explained. "And I certainly don't want to see it happen again."

"Neither do I," he agreed, then leaned forward on the sofa, bracing his elbows on his knees. "I don't know if you've heard, but *The Luna* has some serious damage on one side of her hull."

"I saw it when I was at Friday Harbor earlier today," she told him.

"Some people are saying that *The Luna* hit the mother orca and that's what caused the damage."

"What do you think?"

He hesitated for a long moment, staring at the coffee in his cup. Then he looked up and met her gaze. "I don't think so.

Seth and Margie Anderson seem like good people to me. Besides, why would they do it?"

"The question is, why would anyone do it?" Abby countered. "And how did their hull get damaged? Do you have any ideas?"

He shook his head. "No, but I intend to keep a good lookout from now on. I'm keeping a sailor on board *The Adventurer* twenty-four hours a day. My crew's grumbling about the extra work, but I can't afford not to do it."

Abby assumed he wasn't the only boat captain taking extra security measures. "So you think someone deliberately vandalized *The Luna*?"

Captain Hovel stared at her, then a smile tipped up one corner of his mouth. "Are you sure you're a bird specialist? Because you sure sound a lot more like a detective to me."

She laughed. "I'll admit I like a little mystery in my life."

His smile broadened as he set down his cup on the coffee table. "Then you'll want to hear the real reason I came here tonight."

"The real reason?" Abby echoed, confused by his words.

Captain Hovel set down his coffee cup. "I know who hurt the mother orca."

CHAPTER ❦ SIX

ABBY STARED AT CAPTAIN Hovel. "You know who sailed through the K pod and hit Rosie?"

He nodded, then stood up and began to walk back and forth across the floor. "I don't have any hard evidence, but enough suspicion to convince me who's guilty."

She watched him pace, as if he was unable to contain the energy pent up inside of him. Abby's own heart was pounding in her chest, and she took a deep breath to calm herself.

"Do you know a Captain Dennis Zirka?" he asked, before she had a chance to speak.

Abby shook her head. "I've heard he owns *The Sea Prince*, but I've never met the man."

"I know him only casually." Hovel walked over to the window, his gaze on the starlit sky. "But I hired one of his former crewman last week. It seems Captain Zirka is a hard man to work for."

"Last week," Abby mused. "Then you hired him before the orca pod incident?"

He nodded. "The sailor made it clear why he left Zirka's

employ. Apparently, he's had his boating license revoked before. Zirka doesn't have much respect for maritime law."

Captain Hovel turned to face her. "Doesn't that sound like a man who would sail through a pod? Who would hit an orca and not give it a second thought?"

Abby didn't know what to think. She didn't want to point the finger at Captain Zirka because of his past. She truly believed that everyone was capable of redemption. But had he repented his past actions? Or was he just as reckless as before?

"Like I said," Captain Hovel continued. "I don't have any proof, but if you're looking for someone capable of hurting those magnificent creatures, you should turn your focus on the captain of *The Sea Prince*."

She stood up. "Thank you, Captain Hovel. You've been a big help."

"You're welcome," he replied as he moved toward the front door. "I think I've taken up enough of your Saturday night. And I apologize again for taking your message the wrong way. The only excuse I can make is that it's been a long day and I'm pretty worn out."

"No apology necessary," she assured him. "I enjoyed meeting you."

"Same here," Captain Hovel replied. "I'd still like to make it up to you, though. How about a free tour to go whale-watching on *The Adventurer*?"

Abby considered his offer, deciding it would be a perfect way to take a look at the scene of the crime. "Thank you, I'd like that."

He gave a brisk nod, then reached out to shake her hand. "Good night, Abby."

"Good night, Captain Hovel."

She watched him leave, his figure soon swallowed up in the darkness. He hadn't mentioned any family during his visit and she sensed a loneliness about him, especially when he talked about his difficulty making connections here. She hoped he accepted her invitation to attend services at Little Flock Church.

"Abby?" Mary called from the dining room, breaking her reverie.

"I'm coming," Abby replied, closing the front door. When she returned to the dining room, she saw Henry and her sister waiting at the table for her. "Sorry I took so long."

"No problem," Henry replied. "I've been working with the Coast Guard on the orca pod investigation and frankly, we can use all the help we can get on this one."

Abby took her seat, grateful that she wasn't intruding on his territory. "Does that mean it's not going well?"

He sighed. "We don't have any solid leads, I'm afraid. The Andersons look like the most likely suspects, but they just don't strike me as the type to do such a thing."

"I agree," Abby replied, frustration growing inside of her. But she didn't want to put a damper on their pleasant evening by rehashing the case again. "Is the game over?"

"No." Mary flashed a smile at her beau. "I challenged Henry on the word *fumet* and he told me if I lost I'd have to give him another piece of pie."

"So it really is a word?" Abby asked, looking at Henry's satisfied expression.

"It sure is," he replied. "And Mary just lost her turn for that challenge. Although, her pie is so good I say go ahead and take your turn."

Mary smiled at him. "You're so romantic."

Abby settled into her chair, her mind still on her conversation with Captain Hovel. She wasn't quite sure what to make of the man, though she told herself to keep an open mind. She had to consider him a suspect in this investigation, along with the other boat captains.

Hovel's revelation about Captain Zirka did give her pause. If Dennis Zirka had lost his boat license at one time, the infraction must have been pretty serious. Could he be the one responsible for hitting the mother orca and for damaging *The Luna*?

She still didn't know for certain if the two events were connected. Yet, it made sense that someone had purposely damaged *The Luna* to make it look like the Andersons had caused the injuries to Rosie.

"Earth to Abby," Mary said, waving a hand in front of her face.

She blinked, realizing she'd been lost in her own world. "I'm sorry. I guess I was daydreaming."

"About the handsome Captain Hovel?" Mary inquired. "I took a sneak peek into the living room while you were talking to him."

Abby blushed, though she wasn't attracted to the man at all. Something about him didn't sit right with her, probably his quick temper and defensive demeanor. Nonetheless, she still intended to pursue the information he'd given her tonight.

"Henry," Abby said, looking across the table, "can you do me a favor?"

He looked up from his Scrabble tiles. "Sure, Abby, just name it."

"I'm wondering if there's any information in your police data files about Captain Dennis Zirka, the owner of *The Sea Prince*."

"I can take a look," he replied. "He's one of the boat captains of interest in this case. Is there anything specific that you're looking for?"

"I don't know exactly. Captain Hovel suspects that he's behind the orca pod incident. He hinted that Captain Zirka had previously been in trouble with the law."

"I'll see what I can find out," Henry promised. "Thanks for the tip."

Abby turned her attention back to the tiles in front of her, trying to focus on the game.

"Whose turn is it?" Henry asked. "I have a great word I'm ready to play."

"Better than *fumet*?" Mary teased.

"You'll just have to wait and see," he replied, "but you might want to get your dictionary ready."

As they returned to the game, Abby's gaze moved to the word *fumet* on the board. She'd learned a new word today and met someone new. Only she wouldn't be able to define the man by looking him up in a dictionary. Captain Hovel was just one more mystery that she needed to solve.

THE NEXT DAY, Abby and Mary joined their parents for dinner at the Stanton Farm after church. Abby had been disappointed when she didn't see Captain Hovel among the Little Flock congregation, but she hoped the seed had been planted.

The church pastor, Rev. James Hale, along with his wife Patricia and their two-year-old son Toby, had joined the Stantons for dinner. They all sat at the big oak table, savoring the delicious roast chicken and new potatoes that Ellen had prepared for the meal.

"Where's Sam?" Abby asked as she passed the pea salad to

her sister. The farm's handyman, an ex-convict who had turned his life around, usually joined the family for meals. "I saw him in church this morning."

"He's helping Mrs. Frasier repair a broken step on her front stoop," George explained. "She invited him to stay for dinner since he refused to take any money for the job."

"That's nice of him," Patricia said. "I know Mrs. Frasier values her independence, and taking care of that big old house has been especially difficult since her husband passed away."

Rev. Hale nodded. "It's hard for her to ask for help from anyone. I just keep reminding her that each one of us has talents given to us by the Lord to serve one another. Just as she makes those beautiful quilts that she donates to the Senior Center."

Abby looked around the table, assessing the talents of the people gathered there. Her mother's gift with food and her sister's green thumb. Her father had a special way with people and a love of nature that he'd passed on to both of his daughters.

Her gaze moved to Rev. Hale and she knew that his call to Little Flock Church had been a blessing for all of them. A dynamic speaker, his deep faith and sincerity inspired everyone around him.

His wife Patricia had brought her beauty and vitality to Sparrow Island when she'd left her career as an actress in Hollywood. She was an inspiring woman in her own right and a wonderful mother to little Toby.

As the pleasant dinner conversation hummed around her, Abby found herself looking inward. She hoped her knowledge of birds helped people appreciate the beauty of God's handiwork. Never one to hide her light under a bushel, Abby tried to let God guide her in service to others—wherever that path might lead.

"Who's ready for dessert?" Ellen asked, rising from her chair. "I have spice cake fresh from the oven this morning."

"Good thing I saved a little room, then," Rev. Hale said. "Spice cake is my favorite."

George held up his hand. "Add me to the list."

"And me," Abby and Mary said simultaneously.

"I'll have a small piece." Patricia began wiping Toby's fingers with her napkin. "That was such a wonderful dinner, Ellen. I'd love to have your recipe for rhubarb pickles."

"I'll be happy to give it to you," Ellen replied. "It got handed down to me from my great-grandmother, although I'm not sure I got it exactly right. She used some peculiar kind of shorthand when she wrote down her recipes, so it was difficult to read."

George laughed. "I remember it took Ellen a few tries to get it right. But she finally decoded that recipe, and I've been enjoying it ever since."

"That reminds me," Abby said, reaching for her purse. "Finnegan found a homing pigeon behind the house Friday evening. The bird had a message attached to his leg, but it's in some kind of code."

"How fascinating," Patricia said, as Ellen headed for the kitchen to serve up the spice cake.

Abby passed the coded message around the table. "We don't know where the homing pigeon came from or where he was headed. If we can decipher the message, maybe we can figure out where Homer belongs."

"Homer?" George chuckled. "So you've given the bird a name."

"We had to call him something," Mary said. "The poor little

thing was at death's door when Finnegan found him. But thanks to Abby's tender care and expertise, he seems to be recovering."

Rev. Hale took the note that Abby handed to him. "You know, the early Christians used a form of code to identify themselves to each other by drawing a fish in the dirt. It was one way to avoid their persecutors, yet still enjoy fellowship with one another and spread the Good News."

Abby saw his brow furrow as he looked at the code. "Any guesses?" she asked.

Rev. Hale shook his head. "I'm completely stumped."

Abby watched him pass the note to his wife. "The question I have is why is this note in code? Is it to protect someone in danger? Or is there another, more sinister reason?"

"I had a small part in a film once that featured a coded message," Patricia said, looking at the note in front of her. "In that story, a theft ring was passing information about possible targets."

Abby wondered if she'd recognize criminal intent in the note if she ever decoded it. If so, what then? She supposed she would have to turn it over to Henry to investigate. Though, until she knew where the homing pigeon had come from and his destination, the case might not even be in Henry's jurisdiction.

Patricia passed the note to George. Abby watched her father brush a finger over the bold, black letters and numbers on the note.

"We often used homing pigeons to send messages during the war," he said softly, often reticent to talk about that difficult time. "In fact, I read once that until the invention of the telegraph in 1836, the fastest way to send any kind of news was by homing pigeon."

Abby stood up and leaned over his shoulder. Even at her age, she still believed her father could solve any problem. "Can you figure it out, Dad?"

He sighed, then shook his head. "I don't have a clue, dear. I wish I did. Do you have any idea where the pigeon might have come from?"

"None at all," she replied. "But as Mary said, he's recuperating nicely. I'll be able to send him on his way before too long."

"In the meantime," her father mused, "maybe you should put an ad in the 'Lost-and-Found' section of the newspaper. Even if you're not certain Homer was headed for Sparrow Island, it might be worth a try."

She gave her father's shoulders a warm squeeze, grateful he'd come through for her again. "That's a wonderful idea. I can't believe I didn't think of it myself. I'll pay a visit to *The Birdcall* first chance I get."

Ellen Stanton walked into the dining room with a dessert plate in each hand. "Sorry I took so long. Sam just stopped in to pick up some more tools, and I made him sit down and have a piece of cake. It seems that repairing Mrs. Frasier's step is a bigger job than he thought."

George pushed back his chair. "Shall I invite him to come in here and join us?"

Ellen shook her head as she set dessert in front of Rev. Hale and his wife. "I already did. Sam's in his work clothes and insists that he'll be more comfortable in the kitchen."

Abby moved around the table. "Mom, you sit down and relax. I'll bring in the rest of the cake. You deserve a break after fixing that wonderful dinner."

Ellen smiled. "I never turn down a volunteer."

Abby walked into the kitchen to find Sam seated at the

small table, his stocky body hunched over his plate and one arm curled around it. It was an unconscious habit he'd picked up to protect his food from other inmates during his years in state prison at Walla Walla.

As soon as he saw her, Sam became aware of his prison posture. His cheeks flushed as he immediately straightened and brought both arms off the table.

"Hello, Sam," Abby said, moving toward the counter. Her mother had already dished up each slice of cake. All she had to do was carry them into the dining room.

"Hello, Abby." He dabbed a napkin at the corner of his mouth, then resumed eating his cake. "I just enjoyed a nice dinner with Mrs. Frasier, but I just can't seem to resist your mom's spice cake."

She laughed. "Neither can I."

Abby picked up the remaining dessert plates, carefully balancing them in her hands as she headed out of the kitchen.

"Abby?"

She paused at the threshold, glancing over her shoulder at Sam. "Yes?"

He cleared his throat. "I didn't mean to eavesdrop, but I couldn't help overhearing all of you talking in the dining room. You found a message with a secret code?"

"Yes, I did. It was on an injured homing pigeon. But we can't seem to crack the code."

He fingered the fork in his hand, as if struggling with a decision. "I . . . might be able to help you out there."

A spark of hope lit up inside of her. "Wait here, Sam. I'll be right back."

Abby delivered the rest of the cake as everyone at the table was caught up in a story that Patricia was telling about her days in Hollywood. Then she returned to the kitchen, setting her own dessert plate on the table as she joined Sam.

"I don't want to keep you from the others," Sam said, scooping up his remaining cake crumbs with his fork.

"They won't miss me," Abby assured him. "More coffee?"

He glanced at his empty cup. "Don't mind if I do."

Abby rose from the table and retrieved the coffeepot from the counter. She filled Sam's cup, then grabbed a cup of her own and filled it as well.

She set the coffeepot on the table between them. "Spice cake just isn't the same without a cup of coffee to go with it."

Sam nodded, his gaze fixed on the steam curling up from his cup. "Look, Abby, I might have spoken out of turn before. I'm not really sure if I can help you crack that code or not."

She didn't say anything, sensing Sam's discomfort. Picking up her fork, Abby took a bite of her mother's cake, the piquant flavor melting in her mouth.

"The thing is," Sam said at last, "I do know a guy that does cryptography."

"Cryptography?" Abby echoed. "That's the study of codes, isn't it?"

He nodded. "Codes or ciphers. Walter Endorf is one of the smartest men I know. If he can't crack that coded message, I doubt anyone can."

Abby sensed hesitancy in his tone. "But you're not sure if he'll do it?"

Sam sighed. "I just don't know. Walter might be a smart man, but he did enough dumb things to land himself in prison. He's out on parole now, but he likes to keep to himself."

Abby empathized with Sam's dilemma. He'd found the Lord in prison, but many of his friends had not and were still lost and alone. Some of them wound up back in prison; others just tried to keep a low profile.

She believed everyone deserved a second chance. Sam had gotten his when he was hired on as a farmhand with the Stantons eleven years ago.

"Do you think your friend Walter will talk to me?" Abby asked him. "Or you could take the message to him yourself and see if he can decode it for me."

Sam thought about it for a moment. "It might be best if I go alone. Walter is the shy type. Besides, he'll probably need some time to figure it out anyway. I don't want to take the original, though. Can you make a copy of it?"

"Sure," Abby replied. "I'll make one at work tomorrow and drop it off here after I'm done for the day."

Sam rose to his feet. "Walter lives in Seattle, so I'll take the ferry over sometime this week and let him take a stab at the code."

"Thank you so much, Sam," Abby said, as he set his empty plate and cup on the kitchen counter. "I really appreciate your help."

"Don't thank me yet," he warned her. "This might be a dead end."

"I don't believe in dead ends," Abby replied, "only detours. There's always a way if you look long and hard enough."

He considered her words, then looked up at her with a wide smile. "I think you're right about that, Abby. I've taken a lot of detours in my life, but I sure am glad I ended up here."

She watched him walk out the door, hopeful that his friend could help her solve the mystery held in the coded message. Homer had taken a detour into Mary's backyard. Abby was determined to help the pigeon find his way home again.

CHAPTER ❦ SEVEN

O N TUESDAY MORNING, Abby walked into the office of *The Birdcall* on Kingfisher Avenue, the old-fashioned bell on the door jangling above her. The air had a tang of ink in it, though she knew the presses didn't run until late Tuesday evening.

The weekly paper came out every Wednesday and was the pride and joy of the owner and editor-in-chief William Jansen. Abby saw no sign of him now in the front office, nor anyone else, for that matter.

"Hello?" she called out. "Anyone here?"

There was no answer. Swallowing a sigh of frustration, Abby didn't know whether she should wait for someone to appear or come back another time. Suddenly, she heard the bell behind her and turned to see William Jansen walking through the door.

He scowled when he saw her, then looked around the empty office. "Where is everybody?"

"I don't know," Abby replied. "I just got here myself."

As William sailed past her, she glimpsed an ink spot on his white shirt pocket. He kept a small notebook and pen there and the ink must have bled through.

Now she was in the awkward position of either pointing out the stain and possibly embarrassing him or not saying anything while the stain grew larger. Abby knew if she was in his position, she'd want to know, so she decided to tell him about it.

"William," she began.

"Hold on there a minute, Abby," he replied as he walked through the swinging gate of the counter that separated the front and back offices.

Abby waited, wondering if she should also tell him that she'd seen two of his office staff taking a coffee break at the Springhouse Café on her way here. No doubt he'd find out soon enough.

"Must be a big story breaking somewhere," William said, returning to the front office. "Everybody seems to have flown the coop."

William Jansen lived for the big story. A former CEO, he'd chucked it all to live his dream of becoming a newspaper man. He'd brought some of his hard-edged competitive spirit with him when he'd left the business world to enter the field of journalism.

"Now, what can I do for you?" William asked her.

Abby opened her bag and dug out the advertisement she and Mary had composed during breakfast. "I'd like to put an item in the Lost-and-Found column of this week's paper if it's not too late."

"Certainly." William plucked his bifocals out of his pocket, unaware of the spreading ink stain. "The deadline for this week's edition is at noon, so you even had a little time to spare."

"You have a spot on your shirt," Abby pointed out. "I just wanted to let you know before it gets any worse."

He glanced down at the ink stain, then heaved a loud sigh. "You'd think with all the newfangled inventions and modern technology in this world, someone could invent an ink pen that doesn't leak."

"I've heard hairspray can take out ink stains," Abby suggested.

William pulled the pen from his pocket, then tossed it into the trash can. "Hairspray? Not sure I have any of that on hand. I suppose I could buy a bottle and give it a try. I have several shirts stained just like this one, so I can do a lot of experimenting."

Abby smiled as she handed him the advertisement. "I'm looking for the owner of a lost bird. A homing pigeon, actually."

"We've had a good success rate with our 'Lost-and-Found' column," William told her. "You'd be amazed at how many tourists lose things here on the island. Wallets, jackets, cellular phones. One time someone even lost their false teeth."

"That would be a problem," Abby replied with a smile.

"Well, let's see what you've got here." He slipped the bifocals on his nose, then read her advertisement aloud. "Found: One gray homing pigeon on Sparrow Island. The bird was injured, but is now recovering. Please call Dr. Abby Stanton at the Sparrow Island Nature Conservatory for more information."

"How does it sound?" Abby asked him.

He gave a brisk nod. "Should do the job. I'll put it at the top of the Lost-and-Found section of this week's edition."

"Thank you, William," she said, then turned toward the door.

He circled in front of her to stop her from leaving. "Actually,

I'm glad you stopped in here this morning, Abby. You're just the person I've been wanting to see."

"I am?"

He pulled the notebook out of his ink-stained pocket, then frowned when he searched for a pen. "Oh, that's right. I just threw that one away." He walked over to the counter, picking up a stray pencil and licking the tip as he turned back to Abby.

"I'm writing an article about the orca pod incident that happened last Thursday," William said, "and the search for the missing baby orca. I was hoping you could help me fill in some blanks."

"I'm not sure I have anything new to tell you." She glanced at her watch. "But I do have a few minutes."

"Wonderful." William jotted something down in his notebook. "Now, I was told that you're the one in charge of the investigation.

"Oh, I wouldn't say that," Abby countered. "I'm just concerned about what happened and have checked into a few leads."

The editor flipped back some pages to check his notes. "According to a Mr. Mick Wymore, you've been doing more than that. I met him for breakfast this morning and he gave me quite a story."

Abby was surprised at how quickly Mick was making friends on Sparrow Island. Especially when compared to Captain Hovel's inability to do the same. Then again, Mick did have the kind of charm and personality that made people warm up to him quickly. She hadn't heard from him herself for a couple of days, but presumed he was busy looking for Poppy and studying the pods.

"So do you have any suspects in the case yet?" William asked her.

Abby wasn't ready to convey her suspicions about anyone—especially when she didn't have any proof. "I'm just trying to find out how the mother orca was injured and looking for any information available about the missing baby orca."

"Her name is Poppy, isn't it?"

"Yes," Abby replied. "She's from the same K pod as her mother, Rosie."

He jotted down her reply. "It truly is a shame, isn't it? There's a good chance the poor little thing might not even be alive anymore."

At almost a thousand pounds, a baby orca could hardly be described as little, but Abby shared his sentiment. "I'm still hoping for the best."

He nodded, adding her response to his notepad. "Is there anything the residents of Sparrow Island can do to help find Poppy?"

"Just keep their eyes open," Abby said. "If they see a small orca alone in the water, there's a good chance it's Poppy, since orcas always travel in groups."

He tapped his chin with the pencil. "I wonder if we could get The Whale Museum to offer a reward. Drum up some good publicity that way."

"I think The Whale Museum's resources are already stretched to the limit," Abby replied. "We'll just have to count on the better nature of people to report any information they have, even if there isn't a cash reward."

"Yes, you're right. I told Mick that a story like this can really fire people up."

"I hope so," Abby said. "Orcas are becoming an endangered

species. Even the loss of one of those beautiful creatures is too many."

"*Ooh*, that's a great angle," William said, jotting it down. "I'd love an exclusive on this story, but Mick pointed out that you need to talk to as many reporters as possible for the publicity angle. I guess I can see where he's coming from."

Despite his words, Abby could hear the disappointment in William's voice. His fierce rivalry with the *Puget Sound Sentry* was well-known and no doubt it grated on him to share this story with a newspaper he considered inferior to his own.

"The most important thing right now is finding Poppy and reuniting her with her mother and the K pod," said Abby.

William nodded. "That's why I'm splashing that picture Bobby McDonald took of the baby orca on the front page of *The Birdcall*, above the fold. Mick gave me a copy of it this morning."

Abby knew Bobby would be thrilled to have his photograph published in the newspaper. She hoped the publicity would help widen the search. The longer Poppy stayed lost from the K pod, the less chance she had of surviving.

The bell jangled as the door opened and a diminutive young blonde walked inside.

"Where have you been, Amy?" he asked gruffly. "We've got a paper to run here. That means deadlines, copyediting, typesetting and advertising. The whole nine yards. I can't have my staff gallivanting all over the island when it's time to put it to bed."

Amy smiled, obviously unfazed by his act of playing the tough newspaper man. "I haven't been gallivanting. I've got a big scoop for you."

His eyes lit up. "What is it?"

She glanced at Abby, as if uncertain whether to share this journalistic tidbit in front of her.

"It's okay," William assured the young woman. "This is Dr. Abby Stanton. She's the Associate Curator at the Sparrow Island Nature Conservatory. You can talk in front of her." Then he continued the introduction. "Abby, this is Amy Watts. She's a journalism intern from the University of Washington."

"Nice to meet you, Amy," Abby said.

"Same here." Amy moved closer to them, lowering her voice a notch. "My scoop is about Captain Zirka."

"Dennis Zirka?" William said. "The owner of *The Sea Prince*?"

"One and the same," Amy replied, a mischievous gleam in her eye. "I found out that he sold his boat to Kyle Breslin yesterday."

William's mouth dropped open. "No!"

"Yes," Amy affirmed. "I interviewed Kyle myself when I heard about it." A blush of embarrassment turned her freckled cheeks a becoming shade of pink. "We've sort of dated once or twice. Anyway, Kyle confirmed that the rumor's true."

Abby wasn't familiar with Kyle Breslin or Dennis Zirka. As far as she knew, neither one of them lived on Sparrow Island.

"But Zirka's been running his tour boat out of Friday Harbor for the last ten years," William said. "Dennis loves the water and he's not old enough to retire yet."

Amy shrugged. "All I know is that he called Kyle with an offer to sell on Saturday and they signed all the papers on Monday afternoon."

Abby wasn't a businesswoman, but she understood the implications of this news. "With *The Luna* out of business and Captain Zirka selling his boat to another line, that means less competition in the whale-watch tour boat business, doesn't it?"

William nodded. "And knowing Dennis Zirka as I do, I find it more than a little strange."

Amy leaned even closer. "That's not all. Apparently, Zirka disappeared right after he signed all the legal papers. Nobody knows where he is."

This news had Abby even more intrigued than the sale. Captain Zirka's sudden sale of his boat and his disappearance, combined with his past, made him look very suspicious.

Amy headed toward the back office. "I need to get started writing up this story."

"Go right ahead," William told her, then he turned to Abby. "If you're looking for suspects, this new business merger sounds mighty fishy to me. I'd call on Captain Kyle Breslin and ask him what exactly is going on around here."

ABBY ATTENDED TO HER DUTIES at the conservatory, then grabbed a quick lunch before pursuing her latest lead. If William was right, she was about to add another suspect to her growing list.

Did it all tie together somehow? The injured mother orca. The damaged *Luna.* The sudden acquisition of Captain Zirka's tour boat by Kyle Breslin and Dennis Zirka's subsequent disappearance. Add to that Captain Hovell's allegation that Zirka had a shady past.

Abby just couldn't be sure. Not until she had more information. The only way to find the answers to her questions was to interview anyone who might have had a reason to be near the K pod.

She had to proceed carefully though, or run the risk of offending the people most likely to give her the information she needed—just as Captain Hovel had taken offense at her innocent message.

Abby took a ferry from Green Harbor to Friday Harbor. Then she walked the short distance from the dock to the booking office of *The Polaris*. When she arrived there, Abby found a handyman removing the sign at the front of the building. A new office sign leaned against the weathered wood siding; the words NORTH STAR CRUISES stood out in bright red letters against a navy blue background.

She found it interesting that Captain Breslin already had a new sign waiting to be mounted when, according to the reporter, the deal had only become official yesterday.

Either Breslin was extremely confident in his negotiation skills—or he had some kind of inside information that Captain Zirka would agree to sell.

The window on the booking office was closed, covered by a large piece of plywood to protect it from the construction above. She knocked on the door, hoping to find someone inside.

A young man opened the door, his eyes straining to recognize her. "May I help you?"

Abby briefly took in the young man standing before her. "Yes, I'm looking for Kyle Breslin."

"You've found him." He held out one hand. "Wait a minute, are you Dr. Abigail Stanton? I've heard a lot of great things about you."

She nodded her affirmation, shocked to realize that the owner of North Star Cruises was standing right in front of her, and that somehow he knew her. His wide grin revealed a set of braces, which, combined with the sprinkling of freckles across his nose, made him look more like a teenager than a boat captain.

"Come on in," he said, waving her over the threshold.

Her gaze took in the high flush in his clean-shaven cheeks, then moved past him to see the plastic champagne flutes littering the square wooden table in the middle of the room.

"Maybe I've come at a bad time," Abby said, hesitating in the doorway.

"Not at all," he insisted, ushering her inside. "I was wondering if our paths would ever cross and here you've come right to my door."

Abby searched her memory, but simply couldn't place the young man. The most obvious explanation was that he'd been a visitor at the conservatory and had taken one of her birding tours.

"May I offer you a glass?" he asked, reaching for an open bottle.

She held up one hand. "No, thank you."

"It's just sparkling grape juice," he explained, amusement flashing in his mossy green eyes. "Quite refreshing."

One glance at the label confirmed that the bottles designed to look like champagne were in fact simply white grape juice. On closer inspection, she attributed the redness in his cheeks to windburn and not inebriation, as she'd suspected when she first saw him.

"It looks like you've been celebrating," Abby said, moving further into the room.

"Yes, I have," he replied. "I just made the announcement

about my new boat purchase to the crew. Now they're off getting *The Polaris* ready for the afternoon tour. I hope to have *The Sea Prince* ready to sail by next week. Captain Zirka didn't keep the tidiest ship."

He cleared off the table, then pulled out a chair for her. "Please sit down and join me, Dr. Stanton."

Abby accepted his offer, eager for a chance to find out more about this young man and his growing business.

"Please call me Abby."

"Only if you call me Kyle." He poured a glass of grape juice and placed it in front of her.

"Thank you, Kyle."

He refilled his glass, then lifted the plastic flute into the air. "To North Star Cruises and new opportunities."

Abby took a sip of her grape juice, studying Kyle over the rim of her glass.

He caught her staring and grinned again. "I'll bet you're wondering how I know you."

She set down her glass. "I'll admit I am curious about that."

"Do you remember Roger Harris?"

The name took her back forty years. Roger Harris had been her first crush—a young man who had shown an interest in the studious Abby, until her prettier older sister had taken him away from her.

The old wound had been fully healed recently, helping to bridge the gap that had separated Abby and Mary for so long. But the sudden mention of Roger's name tickled her heart like a feather. She could see his young, handsome face in her mind and remember the emotional upheaval he had caused in her life at such a tender age. Funny how something that had happened so long ago could still be so fresh in her mind.

"Of course I remember Roger," Abby said at last. "We attended school together on Sparrow Island."

Kyle nodded. "I know. I've seen your picture in his yearbook."

"You know Roger?" she asked, wondering what had become of the man who had broken her young heart.

Kyle's grin widened. "He's my father."

CHAPTER ❦ EIGHT

Your father?" abby gasped.

Kyle nodded. "I know we don't look very much alike. I take after my mother's side of the family."

"But you don't . . ." Abby blurted, then stopped herself. In this age of divorce and single parents, it wasn't unusual for a child to have a different last name than a parent.

"Actually, I didn't even meet him until six years ago," Kyle explained, perching himself on one corner of the table. "He and my mother divorced before she knew she was pregnant and she moved to Florida. We lived our own life and when I turned eighteen, I looked him up."

Abby was saddened to hear that Roger hadn't known he had a son. There was no way he could ever get those years back.

"Where's Roger living now?" Abby asked.

"In San Diego. He still gets *The Birdcall* every week, though, and keeps up with all of his old friends. That's how I knew who you were."

The fact that Roger not only remembered her, but had

mentioned her to his son flustered Abby a bit. "What does your father do?"

"He's an architect and runs a big firm. I thought about following in his footsteps and went to college for a while, but I prefer to spend my life outdoors instead of wasting it in a stuffy classroom. Dad was bummed out for a while, but he got over it."

During her time at Cornell, Abby had seen a lot of students like Kyle. Young men and women who chafed at the stressful responsibilities of a college education. Too many of them dropped out without a plan for the future, but Kyle seemed to have landed on his feet.

"So you went from studying architecture to becoming a tour boat captain," Abby mused. "That's quite a transition."

He nodded. "Yeah, Dad bought me this boat when I turned twenty-one. Trying to make up for lost time, I guess. But I sure didn't complain."

"You must be doing well if you're already expanding your line."

"I work hard and it's paying off," he said.

The sound of a hammer banging on the roof reminded her of the new sign outside. "Have you been planning this merger long?"

Kyle considered her question. "Not really. I mean, I told my dad that it would be cool to have a fleet of boats someday. He's been hounding Captain Zirka for months to sell his boat to me, but the guy always refused. Then Zirka calls me one day out of the blue and says he's ready to unload it."

"Did he say why he wanted to sell?"

Kyle shrugged. "Not really. All I know was that the news about the injured orca really got him upset."

One more reason to suspect Captain Zirka. "Do you remember exactly what day he asked you to buy his boat?"

He crinkled his brow. "Let's see, I think it was on Friday . . . no, Saturday. Yeah, it was on Saturday evening, because that's the day my new video game arrived in the mail and I had to wait to play it until we'd worked out all the details of the sale."

His comment reminded Abby of his youth. Running his own business at such a young age was quite an accomplishment, even with his father's financial assistance. "So your father agreed to the purchase?"

"He sure did," Kyle replied. "He didn't seem all that surprised, either. I think Captain Zirka might have contacted him about it before he called me."

Abby wondered if Captain Zirka—fearing that he'd become the prime suspect in the orca incident if his past became public—wanted to get out of the business as quickly as possible.

"Yep, fate certainly smiled on me last week," Kyle said, pouring himself another glass of sparkling grape juice.

At first Abby was confused, then realized he was talking about the orca pod incident.

"My dad always says that one man's folly is another man's fortune," Kyle added.

She opened her mouth to tell him that his good fortune had come at the expense of Rosie and her baby. Then she closed it again, aware that this was no time for a lecture. He might be the same age as her former college students, but Kyle Breslin still had a lot of growing up to do.

He saw her expression and rushed to clarify himself. "Look, I know that sounds harsh, but I'm a businessman, like my father. He never sugarcoats anything. I really do hate what happened to that mother orca and to her missing baby. Everybody's talking about it."

Something told her that despite giving up architecture, Kyle wanted to be a tough businessman like the father he hadn't known growing up. Her irritation with his earlier cavalier attitude turned to sympathy for the boy who was still trying to learn how to be a man.

It also made her wonder about Roger and how much he'd changed since high school. Surely not enough to arrange an *accident* so his son's new business could expand . . .

"So what do people around the marina think happened?" Abby asked, pulling him back to the present.

Kyle hesitated. "I really don't like to spread rumors . . ."

Abby's opinion of him grew. "I don't either. They only hurt people, those who are the victims of the rumors as well as those who spread them."

"There's been quite a bit of nasty gossip about the Andersons," Kyle admitted. "But I like them. They helped me a lot when I first got started here. I just can't believe they'd ever do anything unethical like that."

Abby agreed with him. The little evidence she did have— the damaged hull of *The Luna*—pointed to the Andersons hitting the orca. But it was almost too obvious.

"Do you want to know what I think?" Kyle asked, his gaze meeting hers and not flinching.

"Absolutely."

"I think someone set them up."

Abby thought so too, but she wanted to hear Kyle's reasoning. "Really?"

Kyle nodded. "It all just seems too convenient, you know? Their boat has a big dent in it the day after an orca whale is injured, which they would try to hide if they'd really done it, right?"

He sighed. "It doesn't make any sense. I just wish I knew who was trying to set them up—and why."

So did Abby. There was one person she hadn't interviewed yet who might be able to provide the answer. "Do you know where I can find Captain Zirka?"

Kyle shook his head. "I was expecting him to show up today for the party, but he seems to have disappeared."

Disappointment dampened her spirits. "Maybe he's sick."

Kyle shook his head. "I don't think so. I've been trying to call him all day and he's not answering his phone."

The loud patter of a hammer raining down on the roof made them both look up toward the ceiling.

"You could ask Judd," Kyle said, hitching his thumb toward the ceiling.

"Who's Judd?"

"Judd Peavey. He's the guy who's putting up my new sign. He used to work for Zirka on *The Sea Prince*. There's a rumor that he knows something about the boat that sailed through K pod."

Abby's heart skipped a beat. A witness. That was exactly what she needed to solve this case. "What does he know?"

Kyle threw his hands up in the air. "Your guess is as good as mine. He refuses to talk to me about it, but you could still give it a shot."

ABBY SAT IN THE FRONT PEW of Little Flock Church, letting the quiet solitude fill her soul and drain away the anger and frustration that had built up from her conversation with Judd Peavey.

She couldn't even call it a conversation. The man had refused to talk to her. As soon as he'd heard her mention the injured orca, he'd turned his back on her and started hammering so loudly that further conversation was impossible.

Even thinking about it made her angry all over again. How could he keep that information to himself? Didn't he care about Rosie? Didn't he know that any information he might have could lead to finding Poppy?

Her neck began to ache and she realized that her raw emotions had taken their toll on her body. Her face was warm and flushed, her muscles tight. She'd come to the church to let go of her anger and instead had let it consume her again.

Abby took a slow, deep breath, reminding herself that anger only served to cloud her vision, not help her find answers. She closed her eyes, praying for peace and understanding. And she prayed for Judd, aware that anger toward other people only seemed to build a wall between herself and God.

Her prayer for Judd, sincere and heartfelt, tore down that wall and helped her to understand that his refusal to talk to her might be for a reason she didn't understand. Fear. Confusion. Even misplaced loyalty.

It wasn't up to her to judge him.

She opened her eyes, feeling so much better than she had when she'd left Friday Harbor. The setting sun cast a colorful glow through the stained glass church windows. The serenity she'd sought now filled her from the inside out.

"And the peace of God, which transcends all understanding, will guard your hearts and your minds in Christ Jesus" (Philippians 4:7).

Abby stood up, her heart lighter than when she'd entered the church twenty minutes ago. She was so grateful that she could turn her worries over to God.

She arrived home to be greeted by the spicy aroma of cinnamon in the air and a mischievous smile on her sister's face.

"There you are," Mary exclaimed, rolling toward her as Abby entered the kitchen. "I've been waiting for you to get home."

"Why?" Abby asked, finding her sister's smile contagious. "Do you have some good news or something good for me to eat?"

"Both," Mary replied. "The good news is about the coded message we found on Homer. I promised Bobby I wouldn't tell you about it until he got here."

Abby glanced at the kitchen clock, eager to hear the news. "When will that be?"

"It should be any minute now. He called me from the conservatory to tell me he was on his way."

Bobby volunteered at the conservatory, helping Abby care for the birds she was rehabilitating. He was both conscientious and enthusiastic about his duties, which made him the perfect assistant.

"So how was your day?" Abby asked, shedding her bag.

"Busy. June is the month for weddings, so Island Blooms is hopping. Candace is such a capable manager that it gives me a chance to concentrate on designing bouquets, which is what I really love to do."

Her sister had always been the artistic one in the family. Whether Mary was arranging flowers, decorating her home, or choosing her wardrobe, she'd always had an eye for color combinations that Abby envied.

Even now, Mary looked as pretty and elegant as ever in her rose pink jacket and soft gray slacks, with a string of pearls around her neck. Every strand of her silver hair was in place and her blue eyes sparkled with vitality.

Abby smiled to herself, not surprised that Roger Harris had been enchanted all those years ago. "You'll never guess who I met today."

"Who?"

"Kyle Breslin. He's the owner of *The Polaris*, one of the whale-watch tour boats. And he's the son of Roger Harris."

Mary's eyes widened. "*Roger Harris?*"

"Yes," Abby confirmed. "Talk about a blast from the past."

"No kidding," Mary chimed. "He left Sparrow Island after graduation and that's the last I heard of him." Then concern clouded her sister's face. "Not that I wanted to hear from him."

Abby laughed. "Oh, Mary, that's so far in the past." She reached out and took her sister's hand. "We've come a long way since then, haven't we?"

Mary gave Abby's fingers a warm squeeze, her face shining with relief and love. "A very long way."

A knock on the front door signaled Bobby's arrival and Mary followed Abby into the living room as she went to open the door.

"Did you start without me?" Bobby inquired, walking over the threshold.

"No, I waited," Mary told him. "But it was tough."

Abby looked between the two of them. "I can't stand the suspense any longer. Will one of you tell me the good news about the coded message? Have you deciphered it?"

"Not exactly," Mary said, then turned her wheelchair around and headed for the dining room. "You two follow me."

When Abby reached the dining room, she saw Mary pick up a large, white poster board that had been leaning against the wall.

"I decided it would be easier for all of us to see the message if we weren't all hunched over a little piece of paper," Mary explained, setting the poster board on the table. "So I copied the code onto here in big letters."

Abby studied the three lines of code on the poster board.

ZZ6J1P3H3ZK2W4ZS1X3P2R4K2Q3H1ZS4Y4V2Z
ZN1G2J5V2ZC2W3ZM1Q2H2Y5Z
ZP1R4ZF2D3U1J5ZY2F1ZR2B1U3V2F1H4Z

"It does make it easier to see," Abby said. "I just wish it made it easier to decode."

"Bobby's made some progress in that department," Mary told her. "Haven't you, Bobby."

He nodded his head in affirmation. "I've been doing some research on the Internet about codes and stuff."

Abby knew she could always count on Bobby to help her. "What did you find out?"

"It's really interesting," Bobby said. "There are both written codes and spoken codes. Some people use common words as spoken codes so they can communicate in front of other people."

"Really," Abby said, fascinated. "Give me an example."

"If someone's in trouble, but they're working undercover, they might say a code word like *snickerdoodles*. That could mean the word *help* in their secret code."

Mary laughed. "I think you have snickerdoodles on the brain, kid."

Bobby looked sheepish. "I thought I smelled some when I walked in the house."

"You did," Mary assured him. "But they're still too hot to eat, so you'll have to wait awhile."

"Okay," he agreed. "That'll give me time to tell Abby about dictionary codes."

Abby glanced at her sister, still waiting for the good news. "What's a dictionary code?"

Mary rolled her wheelchair closer to the table. "Why don't you show her, Bobby. Use that textbook on the counter."

Abby watched the boy retrieve her copy of *The Nesting Habits of Migratory Birds* from the counter, wondering how it could possibly help them decipher a secret code.

"Just wait," Mary said, seeing her puzzled expression. "Bobby will show you."

Bobby set the book on the table, then got a pencil and a piece of notebook paper from the drawer. "Dictionary codes have been around for centuries. Some people use actual dictionaries, but to be really tricky you'd want to use just a regular book."

Abby leaned closer as he opened the front cover of the textbook. "I still don't understand what you mean."

"Well, let's say we want to send a secret message to someone." Mary wheeled herself beside Bobby. "Something like: Meet me at the park at ten."

Bobby started flipping pages. "The trick is to find the first word, *meet*, somewhere in this book."

Abby watched him as he searched. A few moments later his face lit up. "Here it is on page sixteen. Environmentalists must *meet* the challenge of saving bird habitats."

He reached for the pencil. "So the code for the word *meet* would be 16.5.3."

Abby still didn't understand. "What do the periods mean?"

"The periods separate the numbers," Mary replied.

"Each number is part of the code," Bobby explained. "Sixteen means the page number, five means the number of lines down from the top, and three means the third word in the sentence."

Abby smiled, finally understanding. "So if I use *The Nesting Habits of Migratory Birds* as a code book, then I know that 16.5.3 means the sixteenth page, fifth line down, third word in the sentence. And that gives me the word *meet.*"

Bobby beamed at her. "That's right! Pretty soon you'd have a whole column of numbers like that as your secret code to spell out a sentence."

Abby looked from the numerical code on Bobby's paper to the poster board at the center of the table. "But the code we found on Homer doesn't look like that."

Bobby shook his head. "No, it's not a dictionary code. At least, not one that I understand. It uses both letters *and* numbers."

"So we're back at square one," Abby said with a long sigh.

"Not exactly," Mary replied. She pulled the poster board closer to her. "When Bobby demonstrated the dictionary code for me earlier today, it got me thinking."

She pointed to the first letter in the code—a *Z.* "What if, like periods to separate the numbers in a dictionary code, this code uses letters to separate the words?"

Abby studied the first line of the code again, trying to understand Mary's point.

ZZ6J1P3H3ZK2W4ZS1X3P2R4K2Q3H1ZS4Y4V2Z

"I suppose there does have to be some way to separate the message into words."

"Yes," Mary agreed. "And notice how the only time there are two letters together, one of them is always a *Z*?"

Abby looked again, surprised she hadn't realized it before. "You're right. Every *Z* has another letter to the right of it, instead of a number."

"I think the letter *Z* is just there to separate the words," Mary said, then turned to the boy. "What do you think, Bobby?"

"I think so, too," he said, flipping his paper over to the blank side and breaking the code apart. "Here, look what happens when we separate the *Z*'s that are next to a letter."

Abby glanced down to see the three lines of code now divided into smaller blocks.

Z Z6J1P3H3 Z K2W4 Z S1X3P2R4K2Q3H1
Z S4Y4V2 Z
Z N1G2J5V2 Z C2W3 Z M1Q2H2Y5 Z
Z P1R4 Z F2D3U1J5 Z Y2F1 Z R2B1U3V2F1H4 Z

"Those do look like they could be words," Abby said, fascinated by the revelation. "Now if we can only figure out what they mean."

"At least this simplifies it for us a little bit," Mary said. "If we can figure out just one word, that will be the first step to breaking the code."

Abby smiled, enjoying the fact that they were working as a team. If Sam could convince his buddy Walter to help as well, she'd finally be able to figure out the mystery behind Homer and his secret message.

"All this decoding has made me hungry," Bobby announced. "Have those cookies cooled off yet?"

Abby and Mary both laughed at his not-so-subtle hint.

"Maybe you'd better stay and have dinner with us," Mary said graciously. "We're having spaghetti and meatballs tonight."

His eyes lit up. "I love spaghetti and meatballs."

"Why don't you call your mother and make sure it's all right if you stay."

He bounded toward the telephone, then stopped and turned around. "Hey, I've got an idea! We can say grace in dictionary code." Then he hesitated. "Do you think God would understand it?"

"God knows every secret of our heart," Abby told him. "But I think we'll say grace the old-fashioned way tonight, if that's all right with you."

He sighed. "Okay. I guess it would take too long to look up all those words anyway. And my stomach keeps growling."

Abby exchanged a smile with her sister, thanking God in her heart that they'd been blessed with such a special neighbor.

CHAPTER ✣ NINE

EXACTLY ONE WEEK AFTER Poppy disappeared, Abby arrived at the conservatory to find several large vans in the parking lot. A few of them had a small satellite dish on the roof and station call letters painted on the sides. She saw television trucks from Seattle, Portland, Vancouver and San Francisco.

"What's going on here?" she murmured to herself as she climbed out of her car.

Abby hurried toward the front entrance of The Nature Museum, slanting her way through the crowd of reporters buzzing around the door. She recognized William Jansen from *The Birdcall* among them. He wore another white dress shirt with a blot of dark blue ink on the pocket, though the camera slung around his neck partially obscured the stain.

"William," she said, taking him by the elbow and edging him away from the pack of journalists. "What's happening?"

He scowled. "That's what I want to know. Somebody told me there was a press conference here this morning. When I advised Mick to get the word out about the missing baby orca, I didn't mean he should invite all these interlopers into *my* territory."

Abby hadn't heard a word about a press conference. Surely this had to be some kind of mistake. Yet, why else were there reporters swarming the conservatory grounds?

"Are you sure Mick's holding a press conference?" She hadn't seen the young marine biologist for a few days and assumed he'd been busy with his doctoral research project. "Here at the conservatory?"

"Positive," William said. "I would have appreciated a little advanced notice, Abby. Especially as I've been on this orca story from the beginning."

"This is the first I've heard about a press conference," Abby said, wondering why Hugo hadn't mentioned it to her. Surely Mick had gained his permission before scheduling this event.

Hadn't he?

Abby wanted to find out. "Excuse me, William," she said, before making her way through the crowd of bustling reporters.

When she reached the front entrance of The Nature Museum, she found it guarded by Wilma Washburn, the conservatory's trusted receptionist, secretary and all around go-to person.

"Oh, hello, Abby," Wilma exclaimed, holding the door open for her. "I'm so glad you're finally here."

"What's going on, Wilma?"

"I don't know for sure. Mr. Baron isn't here yet and that guy told me not to let anyone inside until nine o'clock."

"What guy?" Abby asked, although she thought she knew the answer.

Wilma pointed behind her. "Him."

Abby turned around to see Mick grinning at her. "Hello, Abby. Isn't this a fantastic turnout for our press conference?"

Abby didn't know how to respond. "Mick, what's happening here?"

"A wonderful opportunity," he replied as he headed toward the door, "to put the Sparrow Island Nature Conservatory on the map."

Abby watched him prop open the doors, then wave one hand in the air to catch the attention of all the journalists assembled outside.

"Ladies and gentlemen of the press," he began, his deep voice carrying easily over the crowd, "my name is Mick Wymore. On behalf of the Sparrow Island Nature Conservatory, I want to thank you for coming here today. It is very important to the people of the San Juan Islands and to the conservatory that we get the word out about the tragic incident that happened in the Islands last week."

He paused for dramatic effect and the crowd grew completely silent. Abby glimpsed Hugo in the background and wondered if he was as surprised about this turn of events as she was.

"As many of you may already know," Mick continued, "a large boat rammed through an orca pod last Thursday night—specifically, the K pod—and severely injured an adult female orca named Rosie. This was discovered when she beached herself on Lopez Island."

Murmurs rippled through the crowd and Mick waited until they were silent again before continuing with his story.

"As a marine biologist, I can tell you that most beached whales do not survive the experience. Fortunately, in this case, Rosie was treated and returned successfully to her pod."

Abby watched Mick speak, amazed at how cool and calm he appeared in front of the reporters and all of the cameras. He wore khaki slacks and a navy blue jacket with a crisp white dress shirt underneath. Mick looked more like a movie star than a scientist. No doubt he had what Patricia Hale called a *screen face.*

"But we don't have a happy ending yet," Mick continued, letting the phrase hang in the air as he slowly scanned the crowd of reporters. "The injured orca was a new mother. Her baby, a six-month-old orca named Poppy, was separated from the K pod when it was disrupted by the boat."

A small clamor arose as this detail circulated among them. Watching Mick, Abby was fascinated by his ability to work his audience. He knew when to speak and when to pause, as well as how to use just the right words to add even more drama to the story.

Mick waited until the crowd settled down again to continue. "An orca calf cannot survive for long on its own. They ride alongside their mother to reduce wave resistance. Without that help, they tire easily and don't have the strength or endurance to hunt for food. It's been seven days since Poppy disappeared and time is running out."

Abby glanced at Hugo and saw him moving slowly through the crowd toward where she stood at the front entrance of the museum.

"We're asking for your help," Mick continued, "to save the baby orca. Please, get the word out to your readers and viewers."

"How can they help?" shouted a man from the back of the crowd.

"We believe Poppy is still somewhere in the waters around the San Juan Islands. So if you are in the area, please keep an eye out for a lone orca calf in the water. Or if you have any information about this incident, please contact Dr. Abigail Stanton at the Sparrow Island Nature Conservatory."

Abby blinked, surprised to hear him give her name. But before she could say anything, the reporters started shouting more questions at Mick.

"Do you have any leads yet about what kind of boat disrupted the orca pod?"

"Given the seriousness of the injuries to the mother orca, we can only assume that it must have been a large boat of some kind," Mick replied. "Perhaps a tour boat. We have several leads and suspects, but are not prepared to reveal them at this time."

"Could the pod disturbance have been an accident?" another reporter shouted.

"Highly doubtful," Mick answered. "Especially with a professional boat operator at the helm."

"Exactly how long can the baby orca survive on its own?" asked a female reporter.

Mick flashed her a smile. "Orcas are strong, resilient animals. I'd say that Poppy has a strong chance of survival if we can find her within the next few days or so. After that . . ." His voice trailed off, the unspoken words clear to everyone in the crowd.

Hugo moved next to Abby, arching a silver brow in her direction. "Looks like we're in the spotlight," he whispered.

"Did you know about this?" Abby murmured to him as the press continued to question Mick.

"Mick approached me about going public with the news about the missing orca calf, but I had no idea he had this kind of pull with the media. Judging from some of the big television stations that I see here today, this story could make national headlines."

Abby wasn't sure how that would help them find Poppy, but she couldn't deny that they needed to do something to jumpstart the search.

"At this time," Mick announced to the crowd, "I'd like to introduce the Curator of the Sparrow Island Nature Conservatory, Mr. Hugo Baron. Standing next to him is the Associate Curator, Dr. Abigail Stanton."

Abby stiffened as the bright lights of several television cameras focused on her and Hugo. She heard the whirr of cameras snapping and experienced a twinge of self-consciousness to suddenly find herself the center of attention.

"As advocates for wildlife and the environment," Mick continued, "Mr. Baron and Dr. Stanton are actively seeking any information about the disturbance to the orca pod and the missing baby orca."

Mick turned to Hugo. "Would you like to say a few words?"

Hugo stepped forward to address the press. "Thank you for coming here today. We deeply regret the human interference into the natural habitat of the K pod, as well as the injuries to the mother orca. That's why we're determined to do everything in our power to see that it never happens again."

"Are you talking about criminal charges?" a reporter shouted.

Hugo glanced at Abby, then looked back at the crowd. "The Coast Guard can give you the specifics, but I believe some maritime laws have been broken. At this point, our main concern is locating the missing orca calf and reuniting her with the K pod."

"How do you know Poppy wasn't killed in the boat collision that injured her mother?" shouted another reporter.

Mick stepped forward to answer the question. "There's a picture of a lone orca calf in this week's edition of *The Birdcall*. This photo was taken by an amateur photographer one day after the disturbance to the K pod and we believe it is Poppy. That would be proof that she was still alive."

"What's *The Birdcall*?" asked a woman standing next to William Jansen.

Abby saw the editor scowl as he turned and looked at the young reporter. "That's *my* newspaper."

"Mr. Jansen is the editor of *The Birdcall*," Mick interjected, "which is published every Wednesday on Sparrow Island. I'm sure he'll be happy to answer any questions you may have."

Abby watched as reporters surrounded William, who looked less than thrilled at the attention.

"I want to thank you all for coming here today," Mick said, wrapping up his press conference. "Please don't hesitate to contact me if you have any questions. We will be happy to keep you updated if and when we have any new information."

The reporters started to disperse, careful not to trip over the assortment of black camera cables snaking over the ground. Several of the journalists approached the front entrance, causing Hugo and Abby to escape inside. They quickly made their way to Hugo's office, anxious to avoid more questions.

"Well, that was something," Hugo said. "Mick certainly knows how to command a crowd."

"I can't believe how many reporters are out there," Abby said, walking over to the window.

She saw William walking away from the conservatory,

brushing aside the buzzing reporters like so many pesky mosquitoes. Judging by his gruff demeanor, Abby was sure the editor of *The Birdcall* wasn't about to share his story with his larger competitors.

Mick was still there too. She could see his blond head above a group of admiring journalists, many of them female. His smile flashed for the cameras and she had no doubt that his handsome face would appear on more than one evening newscast.

Hugo joined her at the window, watching all the activity. "Stories like this obviously sell, Abby. A baby separated from its mother, human or animal, will pull at anybody's heart strings."

She knew he was right. Abby just hoped that Mick's press conference today would do more than pluck some heart strings. Maybe it would lead to catching the culprit behind the entire incident.

As if reading her mind, Hugo turned to her and asked, "Any new leads?"

She sighed. "Too many. That's the problem. I've talked with three of the four whale-watch tour boat owners and each one could have a possible motive for sailing through the K pod. I'm trying not to let my emotions influence my opinion, but it's difficult."

Hugo patted her shoulder. "Don't be afraid to let your instincts and emotions guide you, Abby. Sometimes that's the only compass we have in life."

She appreciated his support, but she knew the danger of following her heart instead of her head. She needed solid proof before she accused anyone of injuring the mother orca.

"Mick certainly lets his emotions guide him," Hugo said, watching out the window once more. "You can feel his passion when he speaks. He had those reporters in the palm of his hand."

Abby moved to a chair and took a seat. "I was surprised to hear him give my name as the contact person. Do you suppose we'll have a lot of calls?"

Hugo turned away from the window and moved toward his desk. "Perhaps. We can ask one of the docents to handle the telephone and forward any pertinent calls to you. Most of them will probably be people calling with questions rather than answers."

Abby hoped they weren't overwhelmed. Their first priority was running the conservatory and The Nature Museum. But if even one call helped them locate the baby orca, it would be worth it.

Mick suddenly appeared at the office door, his face flushed with excitement. "Wasn't that an amazing experience? If we're lucky, this story could make headlines all over the world!"

Hugo invited him into his office. "I never expected that kind of turnout."

"Neither did I," Mick replied, still so wired from the press conference that he couldn't stand still. "A friend of mine works for the Associated Press. He's got some contacts in the journalism business, so I told him how I wanted to spread the word about the missing orca calf and it just sort of snowballed from there."

"It certainly caught me off guard," Abby said. "Although you did a nice job with the reporters, Mick. I was impressed."

"As was I," Hugo added.

Mick blushed at the compliments. "Thank you. I hope you don't mind that I acted as the unofficial spokesman for the rescue effort."

Abby knew some people might think it presumptuous, but she couldn't help but admire Mick's enthusiasm for the cause.

"Not at all," Hugo assured him. "Anything to find Poppy."

"Hey, that reminds me," Mick said. "I promised one of the reporters that I'd go to lunch with her so we could do a more in-depth interview. Do you happen to have an extra copy of *The Birdcall* with the orca calf's picture?"

"I believe there are some in the gift shop," Abby told him.

"Thanks." Mick headed toward the door.

As they watched Mick walk out of the office, Abby smiled. "He's certainly full of energy this morning."

Hugo nodded his agreement. "Some people feed off that kind of attention. I have to say I'm very impressed with the way that young man handles himself. Maybe we could use his talent and enthusiasm around here."

"What do you mean?" Abby asked.

Hugo walked around his desk, his hands clasped behind his back. "A man with his charm, who commands that kind of attention, could be a real asset to the conservatory. We could hire him for public relations."

Abby considered the idea. "He is an excellent communicator."

"Exactly," Hugo replied. "If we hired him and put him in charge of publicity, we could increase the number of tourists coming here as well as increase our donations and fundraising."

Despite the obvious benefits of hiring Mick to handle public relations, Abby didn't think he'd be interested. "He's a marine biologist. His home and his work are both on the water."

Hugo nodded. "I know. But something led him here, Abby. Maybe this is the place he's meant to be."

She knew God worked in every person's life, leading them down paths they never imagined. That was certainly true in her experience. Maybe God had a special plan for Mick and for the conservatory.

"Let's not mention anything about it to him yet," Hugo advised. "I want to give Mick a chance to adjust to life in the San Juan Islands and to get to know him better. There's plenty of time to see if he'll be part of the conservatory's future."

Something about that prospect made Abby uneasy, but she kept that feeling to herself. She wanted time to think and pray about it. The passion Mick displayed at the press conference might be reserved for orcas and other sea creatures.

Once the orca mystery was solved, Mick might lose interest in the conservatory all together.

Only time would tell.

CHAPTER ❧ TEN

THE FOLLOWING TUESDAY, Abby took Homer out of his cage in the laboratory to continue his rehabilitation. After dictating the details of the homing pigeon's progress into her microcassette recorder, she slipped it back into the pocket of her white lab coat, then placed Homer on the floor to walk around a bit.

Bobby knelt beside the pigeon, rapt with attention. Homer was progressing nicely and Abby hoped to be able to release him soon.

She just wished she knew more about him—and more about the coded message he'd carried. She still hadn't heard from Sam and was losing hope that his friend would be willing to help her decipher it.

"Homer's getting better, isn't he?" Bobby asked, watching as the bird flapped both of his wings and strutted across the floor.

"He certainly is," Abby replied. "And growing stronger by the day."

She had removed the splint three days ago, pleased to find the dislocation completely healed. Homer was eating well, too, and had gained several ounces.

"I want to be a wildlife rehabilitator when I grow up," Bobby said decisively.

"What happened to your career as a photographer?"

His brow crinkled. "Can't I be both?"

His response made her smile. Bobby was always changing his future career plans according to what his current interests were. "I don't see why not. In fact, I'd say those two careers would make a great combination."

Bobby continued with his tasks of tidying up the lab.

"You have a special talent for animals," Abby assured him. "Homer's always excited to see you."

He looked down to see Homer pecking at the frayed hem of his jeans. "I really like him, too. He's so tame and always looks at me with that funny look on his face—like he knows what I'm thinking."

"It does seem that way sometimes, doesn't it?"

Bobby reached out one finger to gently stroke Homer's soft head. "I wish I could keep him."

Abby could empathize with that feeling. There had been many times when she'd regretted releasing one of her birds back into the wild, even when she knew that was the best place for them. It was impossible not to grow close to the animals she rehabilitated.

"I know, Bobby," Abby said. "But I'm sure Homer's owner is missing him. There are probably other pigeons back where Homer lives that miss him too. He might even have some chicks of his own."

"I wish we knew how to find Homer after we release him," Bobby said. "Just to make sure he got home safe and sound."

Abby wished the same thing. Unlike the other birds and animals she rehabilitated, Homer wasn't going to live in the wild. He had a place to call home somewhere.

If only she could decipher that coded message, then they might be able to identify Homer's owner and contact him or her.

That frustration, along with the fact that Captain Zirka seemed to have disappeared, made Abby close her eyes and turn her troubles over to God. She prayed for patience and peace of mind, certain He could provide whatever she needed.

"Look at that," Bobby exclaimed. "Homer's trying to fly!"

Abby opened her eyes to see the gray pigeon flapping both wings fast enough to lift him a few inches off the floor.

"So he is," Abby agreed with a smile. Her hard work had paid off. Homer was almost fully recovered. "It will be time to send him on his way in a few days. He won't want to be cooped up in that cage much longer."

"Do you hear that Homer?" Bobby asked the bird. "You get to fly back home soon."

The pigeon replied with a series of small coos that made them both laugh.

Abby showed Bobby a few more exercises to do with Homer to help him prepare to fly. Though he was gaining strength each day, she still had no idea how far he would have to fly to reach home. She wanted to make certain his wing was completely healed before they let him venture out in the world.

A soft tapping sound made Abby glance up toward the door. She saw Sam standing in the doorway and invited him inside the laboratory.

"Hope I'm not interrupting anything," he said, looking over at the activity in the brooder box.

There were three newly hatched double-crested cormorant chicks in there that Abby had rescued from an abandoned nest she'd come across while hiking over the weekend. It was close to feeding time and the feisty chicks were starting to demand their afternoon snack.

"Not at all," she replied, rising to her feet. She turned to Bobby. "Will you put Homer back in his cage and refill his water for me?

"Sure," Bobby agreed, always eager to help.

"I'll just be few a minutes, Sam," Abby promised, as she walked over to feed the chicks.

"Take your time," he told her. "I'm in no hurry."

He watched as she prepared the special nutrients for the chicks, laughing as they fought over the food she placed in their beaks.

"They're hungry little things, aren't they?" he commented.

"That's a good sign," Abby said. "It means they're healthy."

After she finished up in the laboratory, Abby led Sam to her office. Though she assumed he was here about the coded message, she didn't want to get her hopes up too high. He might be here to tell her that his friend Walter had refused to help decipher the code.

"Well?" Abby asked, unable to wait any longer. "What did he say?"

Sam sighed. "Walter doesn't want to get involved. He's afraid it might be connected to something criminal and that could interfere with his parole."

Her heart sank, even though Abby understood the reason for his reticence. "So that's it then."

"Not exactly. I found someone else who's willing to help you."

She looked up at him, surprised. "Someone else?"

"Walter's kid sister, Peggy, is arriving at The Dorset this evening. She's from Vancouver, but she had a vacation planned here or something."

Abby slipped out of her lab coat and placed it over the chair. "And you think she'll be able to help me figure out the message?"

Sam nodded. "Peggy Endorf is almost as good at deciphering codes as her big brother. He taught her everything she knows."

Abby retrieved the coded message from the top of her desk. "Do you think she'll see me?"

"She's expecting you tomorrow afternoon," Sam informed her, then cleared his throat. "Actually, she's expecting both of us, but I'm not sure I can make it."

Abby was surprised to see a flush of embarrassment in his cheeks. "Oh?"

He swallowed. "Well, the thing is . . ." His voice trailed off as he tried to find the right words. "Peggy is . . . well, she's . . ."

Abby had seldom seen Sam look so ruffled. "Is there a problem?"

His flush deepened. "Peggy's a nice kid, but she's a little too . . . high-strung for me. Plus, for some strange reason she seems to think I'm interested in her . . . romantically."

Abby tried not to smile at this reluctant confession. It also made her all the more curious to meet Peggy Endorf. "So you'd rather I go to The Dorset alone?"

Relief washed over his face. "I sure would, Abby. That is, if you don't mind too much."

"That's fine with me, Sam," she assured him as she walked toward the door. "I appreciate you setting up this meeting. I can't wait to find out what's behind this secret message."

"I hope Peggy can figure out that code for you," Sam said, following her out of the office. "She can get . . . distracted at times."

"I'll take any help I can get."

Abby stepped into the laboratory for a moment to make certain Homer was back in his cage without any problems. Bobby had already left and the gray pigeon was dozing contentedly on a pile of cedar wood chips after his workout.

She folded the coded message and placed it in her bag. If everything went well at The Dorset tomorrow, Homer's secret would soon be revealed.

THE NEXT DAY, Abby walked into the elegant lobby of The Dorset, surprised to find a crowd milling there. June was the beginning of the busy tourist season, but she'd never seen the hotel this congested with people in the middle of the week.

It made her glad she'd dressed up for work today, wearing a dark green silk blouse and gray slacks. She had felt overdressed at the conservatory, however, here at The Dorset she fit right in.

Located on Primrose Lane, The Dorset catered to upscale clientele who wanted to be pampered during their stay on Sparrow Island. It featured a day spa and rich furnishings that were the epitome of luxury.

Abby padded over the soft Persian rug, taking a circuitous route through the guests gathered there and headed toward the front desk. She saw luggage carts piled high with suitcases and a frazzled bellman rushing to keep everything in order.

"May I help you?" asked the clerk behind the check-in desk. He wore a crested navy blue jacket and a harried expression.

"I hope so," Abby replied. "I'm looking for Peggy Endorf. I believe she's a guest here."

"Along with half the Pacific Northwest," the clerk commented. He turned to his computer and began tapping at the keyboard. "Can you spell the last name for me?"

"E-N-D-O-R-F," Abby complied.

The clerk frowned at his monitor. "Ahh, yes."

His tone reminded Abby of her recent conversation with Sam. Both men seemed to have the same reaction to Peggy Endorf.

"Yes, she is a guest at The Dorset," the clerk told Abby. "Would you like me to ring her room?"

"Please," Abby replied, more curious than ever now to meet the mysterious Miss Endorf.

The clerk picked up the telephone receiver and punched in some numbers. A moment later, he said, "Miss Endorf, this is the front desk—"

He stopped talking, his mouth thinning at whatever he heard at the other end of the line. "I'm sorry, we don't have any contour pillows. Yes. I know about the pinched nerve in your neck. You mentioned it when you checked in."

Abby glanced behind her and saw a line starting to form. She wondered if the hotel was hosting a convention this week.

"Miss Endorf," the clerk said into the receiver, his voice louder now, "there is someone here who wishes to see you."

She saw him cup his palm over the mouthpiece. "May I have your name, please?"

"Abby Stanton," she replied.

"Abby Stanton," he repeated into the phone. "What's that?"

She heard him sigh as he placed his hand over the mouthpiece once more. "Are you a masseuse?"

"No," Abby said. "I'm an ornithologist."

"Oh." He blinked, then turned back to the phone. "She's not a masseuse, she's an ornithologist." He listened for a moment, then frowned into the phone. "No, I believe that's a bird specialist, not a back specialist."

Abby heard some impatient rumblings from the people in line behind her and leaned toward the desk. "Tell her that I'm a friend of Sam Arbogast. I'm here about the coded message."

The clerk's eyebrows popped up, but he relayed her information to Peggy Endorf. Then he hung up the phone with a sigh of relief. "Miss Endorf said she'll be happy to see you."

Abby watched the clerk jot Peggy's room number down on a slip of paper.

"Her room is on the third floor." He handed the room number to her. "Good luck."

She did a double-take at his words. Judging from his expression and the phone conversation she'd overheard, Abby assumed that Walter's sister must be a difficult guest.

"Thank you," she said, then headed toward the elevator.

She had to wait several minutes for it to open, then found herself wading inside with a handful of other people. Abby found a spot in the back corner, accidentally bumping against another woman who looked about ten years younger than Abby and was wearing a green sundress.

"Sorry if I'm crowding you," Abby said.

"No problem," the woman responded. "We're in close quarters here. I didn't realize all the hotels in the San Juan Islands were so busy during the summer. I was lucky to find a room at all."

"What floor?" asked a young woman next to the elevator button panel. She looked to be about twenty, with red hair and an array of freckles sprinkled over her pale face. She wore a pair of denim shorts and white T-shirt with the words *SAVE POPPY!* printed across the front in bright yellow and orange letters.

"Three, please," she called out.

The redhead pushed the button for the third floor. "Hey, that's where I'm going, too. Are you here for the vigil?"

"Vigil?" Abby said in confusion.

"Yeah," the girl replied. "The candlelight vigil for Poppy tomorrow night."

She'd been so busy lately, Abby had fallen behind on the news. "There's a vigil?"

The girl rolled her eyes, like the answer should be obvious to anyone with half a brain. "Yeah, for the baby orca. Tomorrow night will be the two-week anniversary of the day she went missing."

"I think you and I are the only ones who aren't here for the vigil," said the woman standing next to Abby. "Did you come to Sparrow Island for business or pleasure?"

"I live here," Abby explained as the elevator began to move. "My name is Abby and I work at The Nature Conservatory."

"How fascinating," the woman said. "I'm Teresa."

"Nice to meet you, Teresa," Abby said, unable to shake her hand because of the close quarters. "What brings you to the island?"

"I'm here for a reunion," she said, as the elevator dinged when it stopped on the second floor. "This is where I get off."

Abby made room for her to exit, noting that two more people got on to make it even more crowded. They wore the same T-shirt as the young woman.

"Hi, I'm Leann," said a woman next to Abby. "I'm so excited about the vigil tomorrow. It's going to be awesome."

Another woman, wearing a designer business suit and carrying a briefcase in her hand, joined in the conversation. "Hi, I'm Roberta. I just got here today. The ferry was so crowded, I wasn't sure they'd get everyone on."

"That's why all these people are here?" Abby inquired. "For the candlelight vigil?"

"That's why my wife dragged me to this place," grumbled a man next to Leann. "I had tickets to the Mariners game. Instead, she wants to spend the week sitting on some boat so we can find this missing orca baby. Like that's going to happen."

"It could," the redhead interjected. "I mean, Poppy has to be somewhere, right? With all these people looking for the poor little thing, we're bound to find her."

The elevator dinged and Abby saw that she'd reached the third floor. The redhead bounded out ahead of her, then waved to Abby as she walked down the hall. "See you at the vigil!"

Abby waved back, amazed that Mick's press conference had generated this kind of response. They'd gotten several calls at the conservatory in the past week, but she'd never expected people to actually come to Sparrow Island to look for the missing orca calf themselves.

When she reached the door to Peggy's room, she lifted her hand to knock, but it swung open before she made contact.

A large blonde stood on the other side. "Are you Abby?"

"Yes," Abby replied, "and you must be—"

Her words were cut off when the woman grabbed her by the elbow and yanked her inside. "Hurry, before they see you!"

"Before who sees me?" Abby gasped, as the door slammed shut behind her.

"The thugs who wrote that coded message!"

CHAPTER ❦ ELEVEN

WHAT THUGS?" ABBY ASKED, as Peggy leaned against the door with one eye plastered against the view port.

"Quiet!" Peggy commanded. "You might have been followed. I don't want them to hear us."

"Followed?" Abby whispered, perplexed by Peggy's behavior. "What makes you think I was followed?"

Peggy turned toward Abby and rolled her eyes. "The coded message, of course. The kind of mind that wrote it . . ." She shivered. "I don't even want to think about what that message might mean."

Abby's pulse quickened. "So you were able to figure it out? You broke the code?"

"Easy as pie." Peggy stepped away from the door, obviously reassured that the coast was clear.

"What did it say?" Abby asked.

Peggy's gaze narrowed on her. "Wait a minute. How do I know you're really who you say you are?"

Abby reached for her purse. "I can show you my identification—"

"Hold it!" Peggy cried.

Abby froze, wondering what she'd done now. No wonder Sam had asked to bow out of this meeting. Peggy played the drama queen role to the hilt.

Peggy held out her hand. "Give me your purse. I'm not about to let you pull a gun on me."

"I don't have a gun," Abby assured her, handing over the bag. "But you can find my driver's license in the brown leather billfold inside."

Peggy pulled out the billfold, flipping it open to reveal Abby's driver's license. "Abigail Stanton," she read aloud. "Brown hair. Brown eyes. Five foot three inches."

Peggy arched a skeptical brow as she looked Abby up and down.

"Are you staying at The Dorset or one of those darling little bed-and-breakfast places I read about in the brochure?"

"I'm not a tourist," Abby clarified. "I live here on Sparrow Island."

"You do?" Peggy clucked her tongue in amused consternation. "Well, that Sam sure is a sly one. He never said a word about you living here. I just assumed you were one of those traveling orthopedists."

"Ornithologists," Abby clarified. "I used to live in New York, but I grew up here and now I'm back for good."

"Well, I'm not surprised he didn't mention it." Peggy giggled like a school girl. "That man gets so tongue-tied around me. I think he has a little crush. Not that I'm complaining, mind you. I absolutely *adore* the strong, silent type."

Abby knew instinctively that Peggy wasn't Sam's type at all.

She had an overwhelming personality that probably had him running for the hills.

"Anyway," Abby said, hoping to steer the conversation back to the subject that had brought her here. "About that coded message."

"Yes, the message." Peggy tapped her forehead with her index finger. "I've got it all up here."

"You memorized it?"

Her eyes widened. "My brother always told me that a good memory will keep you from getting into trouble."

That's not what Abby wanted to hear. "Do you really believe the contents of that note are related to some kind of illegal activity?"

Peggy moved toward the antique oak dresser. "What else could it be?"

Abby shrugged. "I have no idea. But if it is criminal, I suppose I should turn it over to the police. They'd be the best ones to handle something like that."

Peggy pulled open the top drawer of the dresser and retrieved the photocopy of the coded message that Abby had given to Sam over a week ago.

"It's not my place to tell you what to do," Peggy said. "But please don't mention my name if you do go to the police. There could be . . . repercussions."

"What kind of repercussions?"

"Well, my brother was in prison. You know how the police are always so quick to judge." She handed Abby the note. "I hope you know what you're getting into with this, Dr. Stanton. If it were me, I'd probably burn the thing and be done with it."

Abby looked down at the note, but to her surprise, it looked exactly the same as it had when she'd given it to Sam. "You didn't decode it?"

"Of course I did," Peggy replied. "But I already told you that it's all in my head."

"So what does it say?"

The woman furrowed her brow. "Let's see . . . it was something about a meeting. Yes, a secret meeting at some secret place. I'm a little fuzzy on the details at the moment, but it all sounded quite shady to me."

This wouldn't do at all. Abby needed to know the exact message to figure out what to do next. "Could you show me how to decode it?"

Peggy frowned and checked her watch. "I only have a few minutes until my hair appointment, but I suppose I could give you the basics."

Abby held the note out to her. "I'd really appreciate it."

Peggy sighed, then took the note and placed it on the table by the window. "Okay, this code is really pretty simple to figure out. All you need to know is the alphabet and how to count."

"Does the letter *Z* separate each word?" Abby asked her.

Peggy nodded. "Yes, the *Z* is known as an indicator. In this case the indicator is used to mark the beginning and end of each word."

Abby knew Mary would be thrilled to know she'd solved part of the code's puzzle. She couldn't wait to go home and tell her.

"But the letter *Z* can also be used as part of the code," Peggy continued. "That's why there's a double *Z* at the beginning of this code. The first *Z* is the indicator that signifies the start of a new word. The second *Z* tells part of the first letter."

Abby was confused. "What do you mean by *part* of the first letter?"

"Here," Peggy plucked a pencil off the desk. "I'll show you."

Abby leaned closer, eager to learn. She knew Bobby and Mary would both want to know how to crack this code, too, since they'd all been involved from the beginning.

"The first word in the code is Z Z6J1P3H3." Peggy explained. "Ignore the first Z, because that indicates the start of a new word. Now look at the second Z, then the number after it. That combination will give you the first letter."

"So the first word is Z6J1P3H3," Abby said aloud. "I'm sorry, but I still don't understand."

Peggy heaved a sigh of exasperation. "The number tells you that the correct letter is either six spaces forward from the Z or six spaces back."

"But there are no letters after Z."

"That's true," Peggy agreed. "But some codes just start the alphabet over again, so the sixth letter after Z would be the letter F. Six spaces forward after the letter Z is A – B – C – D – E – F."

Excitement rushed through Abby as the code was finally becoming clear. "So the first letter in the first word of the code is an *F*?"

"No," Peggy replied. "This particular code goes backward. The first letter in the first word of this note is *T*."

Abby studied the note, realizing that now that she had the key it would only be a matter of time until she knew exactly what it said.

"So then the next letter is an *I*," Abby said, "because that's one space back from the letter *J*."

Peggy slapped her on the back. "You've got it, girl."

Abby started to figure out the next letter, but Peggy picked up the coded message on the table and shoved it in Abby's bag.

"This has been fun, but I've got to get to the salon," Peggy said cheerfully. "I want to look my best at the vigil tomorrow night. Mick Wymore will be there along with lots of television cameras."

"Mick will be there?" Abby asked as Peggy propelled her to the door.

"Of course he'll be there," Peggy replied. "He's the one who organized it."

Abby wondered why he hadn't told her about it. "Where's this candlelight vigil going to be held?"

"Near The Whale Museum in Friday Harbor." Peggy grabbed her camera off the desk. "That Mick sure is a hunk and a half. I just hope I'm not too late to get a spot at the front of the crowd."

Abby followed her out the door and into the hotel lobby. Other guests were crowded at the elevator, many of them wearing a *SAVE POPPY!* T-shirt just like she'd seen earlier.

Her impatience grew as she waded through the crowds of people on her way out of the hotel. She couldn't wait to get home and decode the message.

The time had finally arrived to reveal Homer's secret.

ABBY FOUND MARY SITTING on the deck behind the house when she arrived home.

"Are you ready to play detective?" Abby asked her, pulling the note from her bag.

Mary's blue eyes widened. "Don't tell me you've cracked the code?"

"With the help of Peggy Endorf." Abby sat down in the

chair next to Mary. "Walter didn't want to get involved, so he sent his sister instead. I met her at The Dorset this afternoon. She's a very interesting woman."

Mary smiled. "Yes, I've heard Sam mention her once or twice before."

Abby unfolded the note, smoothing the wrinkled paper on her lap. "Peggy only helped me decipher the first two letters, so we'll have to do the rest on our own."

"Okay," Mary replied, "but let's get Bobby over here first. He won't want to miss this."

"Good idea," Abby replied. "You call him while I find some paper and pencils. This decoding process is going to take a while."

Mary retrieved her cellular phone from her pocket while Abby headed into the house. Abby could smell the savory aroma of French onion soup and fresh-baked bread as soon as she opened the door.

But her eagerness to find out what was in that note overcame her appetite. Dinner would have to wait while they cracked the secret code.

She returned to the deck with notepads and pencils only to find Mary still chatting on the phone. The snatches of the conversation she heard told Abby that her sister wasn't talking to Bobby.

When Mary ended the conversation, she turned to Abby. "Bobby will be here soon. That was Janet on the phone just now. Did you know there's a candlelight vigil for the missing baby orca at The Whale Museum tomorrow night? Janet's planning to go."

Janet Heinz had been one of Mary's best friends since grade school and was now the secretary at Little Flock. Since moving back to Sparrow Island, Abby had become friends with her, too, and knew Janet couldn't resist helping out with a good cause.

"I heard about the vigil when I went to see Peggy at The Dorset this afternoon," Abby replied. "That's the main reason she came here. In fact, the hotel was packed with tourists wearing SAVE POPPY! T-shirts. I met one couple who traveled from Utah just to participate in the search."

Mary shook her head in amazement. "I saw those T-shirts today too, but didn't realize there'd be a vigil. I can't believe how fast and far this story has traveled."

"Neither can I," Abby admitted. "Hugo was certainly right about Mick. He truly does have a talent for public relations if this candlelight vigil is any indication. I'm just not sure how all this publicity's going to help us find Poppy."

"People are talking about her everywhere," Mary said. "At Island Blooms and the grocery store. I even heard a commentator mention it on one of those talk radio shows. Everyone's pulling for her."

"I just hope they aren't disappointed," Abby said, trying not to despair. Despite the buzz, they were no closer to discovering Poppy's whereabouts.

A loud shout made Abby look up to see Bobby bounding across the backyard. He hurdled over a small rose bush, his arms pumping as he raced toward them.

The young boy was out of breath by the time he climbed onto the deck. "You didn't start . . . the decoding . . . without me, did . . . you?"

Mary laughed. "I told you we'd wait until you finished your dinner. You must have eaten in record time."

He nodded, his chest heaving. "I . . . did. My dad said he's never ... seen me clean ... my plate so ... fast before. Good thing ... it was ... franks and beans. That's one ... of my ... favorites."

"Sit down and catch your breath," Abby advised, handing him a sheet of paper and a pencil. "All we know so far is the first two letters of the first word. There's plenty of decoding left to do."

Bobby took a couple of deep gulps of air, then seemed to recover. "This is so cool. We're actually breaking a secret code."

Abby experienced a twinge of doubt at involving Bobby in the decoding process. What if Peggy Endorf was right about it being a criminal matter?

Then again, Bobby had been involved almost from the beginning. Better to face the truth head on than keep him in the dark and let his vivid imagination take over. Besides, his diligent care of Homer gave him a right to be here.

"I think we're ready," Mary announced, the notepad at the ready in her lap.

"First I'll show you how to solve the code," Abby said. She explained the deciphering process that Peggy had shown her.

"That's so easy!" Bobby exclaimed. "I can't believe I couldn't figure it out before."

"It seems easy now that we know the system," Abby agreed. "But who knows how long it might have taken us to figure it out without an expert to help us."

"Shall we start decoding the note?" Mary asked eagerly.

"Why don't we each take one line," Abby suggested. "You can take the first line, Mary. Bobby can take the second. I'll take the third."

"We can make it a contest to see who gets done first," Bobby announced, a grin of anticipation on his face.

"Count me in," Mary said, her pencil poised at the ready. "I'll have a head start since we know the first two letters are *T* and *I*."

"Okay, everyone," Abby began, handing out a photocopy of the note to each of them. "Ready . . . set . . . GO!"

For several minutes, the only sound was the furious scribble of pencils on paper, accompanied only by the melodious background music of birdsong emanating from the trees.

"Done," Bobby announced first, putting down his pencil with a flush of pride.

"I'm almost there," Mary said, her brow pursed in concentration as she leaned over her notepad.

"Me, too," Abby added as she began deciphering the last three letters in her part of the code. "There. I've got it."

She looked up to find Bobby and her sister both looking at her expectantly. "Everybody ready?"

They both nodded, then Mary cleared her throat and read the first line of the note. "*Time is running out.*"

Bobby read the second line. "*Meet at loft.*"

Abby's heart quickened as she finished the message by reading the third line. "*On date we parted.*"

Bobby wrinkled his nose. "What does that mean?"

Abby put the three phrases together. "Time is running out. Meet at loft on date we parted."

Mary breathed a soft sigh. "I think it's a love letter."

"This cool coded message is a love letter?" Bobby shuddered. "Ugh."

Abby laughed at his response, even as her heart was touched by the subtle longing in the message. "I'm not sure what Peggy may have read between the lines, but it doesn't sound criminal to me. Although the part about time running out does sound a little ominous."

Mary leaned forward in her wheelchair. "Abby, we have to do something. We have to get this message Homer was carrying to its recipient."

Abby chewed the inside of her lip, considering their limited options. "We still don't have a name or a destination. You know, a loft is the name of the place where homing pigeons are kept, but I'm not aware of any such place around here. Are you?"

Mary slowly shook her head. "You would know better than I."

"It's possible Homer wasn't even heading to Sparrow Island when he got sidetracked by that storm." Abby never liked to admit defeat, but she didn't know what to do next. There hadn't been a single response to the ad she'd placed in *The Birdcall* about a missing homing pigeon. And now that they'd decoded the mysterious message, they weren't any closer to discovering who sent it.

"Maybe we could send our own message," Bobby piped up.

They both turned to look at him. "What do you mean?" Mary asked.

"Homer's almost better," Bobby continued. "Right Abby?"

She nodded. "He's getting stronger every day. If we release him, he'll most likely return to where he came from."

"So we could send a message along with him explaining what happened," Bobby said, his face bright with excitement.

"What a great idea, Bobby," Mary exclaimed. "Then at least the person who wrote this note will know why the meeting at the loft never took place."

Abby looked between the two of them, their excitement fueling her own. "Let's do it."

CHAPTER ❦ TWELVE

THE NEXT DAY, ABBY WAS glad she had something to distract her from the situation with Homer. While they had already written another note to place in the tube he carried on his leg, it would be at least another day, maybe two or three, before the homing pigeon would be ready to fly again.

So this was the perfect time to take Captain Hovel up on his offer of a complimentary whale-watching tour on his boat. She was glad he hadn't forgotten about it and had even promised that he'd take her by the K pod when she'd called to make her reservation for today's tour.

Her investigation into the orca incident had stalled since Captain Dennis Zirka was still nowhere to be found. She'd contacted Kyle Breslin again, but he hadn't heard from Zirka. Abby needed to jump-start the investigation again and what better way than to view the scene of the crime?

It was a perfect day to be out on the water. The June weather was a balmy eighty degrees, which almost made Abby feel too warm in the khaki jacket she wore. But she knew that once they started to sail, she'd be grateful for the extra layers to keep her warm from the cool breeze off the water.

The boardwalk was thick with tourists as she headed toward the marina at Friday Harbor where *The Adventurer* was docked. She sidled through the crowd, enjoying the happy chatter all around her.

People were always awed by their first visit to the San Juan Islands. Even though Abby had grown up here, she still appreciated the pristine beauty of nature that surrounded them.

Some island natives grew weary of tourists, but Abby liked experiencing the islands through their eyes. Glancing at her watch, she saw that there was still plenty of time before she was due to board *The Adventurer*. Eager to see an old friend, she made a detour toward Barney's Gourmet Hot Dog cart.

She found him in the same spot he'd occupied before, the damaged *Luna* still docked behind him. A long line of customers wound around his cart. Abby joined them, patiently waiting her turn.

Barney grinned when he saw her, then gave her a wink as he expertly slipped a roasted footlong into a bun. The savory aroma in the air made Abby's mouth water. She was tempted to buy a hot dog, but she'd already packed a cold lunch for the boat tour.

"I see my fantastic foot longs have lured you back here," Barney teased when Abby reached the front of the line. "Are you ready to try a turkey dog on a whole wheat bun today?"

"They smell delicious," Abby told him. "But I'll have to take a raincheck. All I need today is a bottle of water. I'm headed out on *The Adventurer* in a little while."

"Off to see the orcas, eh?" Barney asked her as he retrieved a bottle of chilled water from his cooler.

"That's right."

"Well, you sure won't be lonely. In my fifty odd years in the business, I've never seen this place so busy. That missing baby orca is sure keeping me hopping."

"Maybe you should think about taking on an assistant," Abby suggested, hoping the octogenarian wasn't working too hard.

He chuckled at her concern. "Nah, it's good for me. Keeps this old man on his toes. Besides, I like meeting all these good folks."

She handed over her money, then took the bottle of water from him. "I like that part of my job, too."

"I can tell," Barney told her with a smile. "You've got a special sparkle in your eyes that reminds me of that little girl in pigtails who used to run up to my hot dog cart."

Abby blushed at the compliment, then moved aside so the couple behind her could place their order. Glancing at her watch, she saw it was nearly time to get over to *The Adventurer*.

"Don't leave yet," Barney told her. "There's something I need to tell you."

She waited while he finished serving all of his customers, noting more than one *SAVE POPPY!* T-shirt among them. Her schedule made it impossible for her to attend the candlelight vigil this evening, but she had made a lunch date with Mick for tomorrow. They had a lot of catching up to do.

"Sorry for the long wait," Barney said, wiping his hands on a clean dishtowel. "Looks like I have a short reprieve before the next rush."

"No problem," she said. "I have a few more minutes to spare before it's time to board."

He nodded. "Well, I just wanted to tell you that I'm still working on Judd Peavey to tell us about what happened that night."

She swallowed a sigh of frustration, remembering how the recalcitrant sailor had refused to answer any of her questions about the disturbance to the K pod. "I hope you have better luck with him than I did. The way he scampered up that roof the day I tried to talk to him, you'd think he was afraid I was going to propose marriage."

Barney laughed. "Judd is a stubborn fellow, but I'm even more stubborn. Patient, too. Just give me some time, Abby. I'll make him come around."

Abby thanked him, then bid Barney good-bye and headed for the boarding gate of *The Adventurer*. It was time for her to get an up-close and personal look at Rosie and the K pod for herself.

CAPTAIN HOVEL MET ABBY as she climbed up the steps to the boat. "I'm so glad you could make it today, Abby," he said, reaching out a hand as she stepped onto the deck. "Welcome aboard *The Adventurer*."

"Thank you," Abby replied, accepting his assistance. "I hope we'll see some orcas today."

"I can guarantee it," Captain Hovel said. "I sent my whale spotters out this morning and they found a prime location for us to view the K pod."

"Wonderful." Abby's gaze wandered around the deck, which was rapidly filling with people. She hoped she could find a good spot at the rail. The seats were already taken on both the upper and lower decks.

"We're not due to launch for few more minutes," Captain Hovel said. "May I give you a tour of my pride and joy?"

"I'd like that very much," Abby replied, eager to learn more about *The Adventurer*. Just a quick glance around the boat told Abby that Captain Hovel and his crew kept the boat in tip-top condition. There was certainly no indication that it had rammed into an orca.

As Abby accompanied Captain Hovel around his vessel, she was left with no doubt that *The Adventurer* truly was his pride and joy. He spoke of his boat like a parent telling her about his favorite child, love and admiration reverberating in his voice.

"She can cruise up to thirty-six knots fully loaded," he said, leading Abby into the engine room, "and is the fastest boat I've ever had the pleasure to own."

"Does the noise from the engines ever bother the sea animals?" Abby asked.

He shook his head. "No, these jet drives under the surface are both quiet and safe for the animals living there. *The Adventurer* was designed by one of the best marine architects in the business."

"It is impressive," Abby said, as he led her out of the engine room.

"If you want impressive, take a look at this pilothouse." He led her into another small room. "She's got all of the state-of-the-art equipment. There's an underwater microphone for listening in on the orcas, complete with a full stereo system."

"That is impressive." Abby was intrigued by the advanced technology. "So will we be able to hear the orcas communicate with each other underwater?"

"If we're lucky." He turned to the opposite wall. "And here's our public address system to talk with our guests. I employ a naturalist who gives running commentary at various points throughout the tour."

"It looks like you have all the right equipment for a great tour."

"And I haven't even mentioned all the amenities," he continued. "There's a heated guest cabin in case you get chilled on the ride and—"

His speech was cut short by the arrival of one of the crewman.

"Excuse me, Captain," the sailor said from the open doorway.

Captain Hovel frowned at him. "What is it?"

"Just thought you'd want to know that the number two engine is ready to go."

He gave a brisk nod. "Fine."

The sailor hesitated a moment, as if he wanted to say something else, then turned around and disappeared.

Abby felt a twinge of sympathy for the young man and wondered if the captain was that brusque with all of his crew. She knew seamen who believed in running a tight ship, but Captain Hovel's tone and manner toward that sailor had bordered on rudeness.

"I apologize for the interruption, Abby," Captain Hovel said. "Now, where was I?"

"You were telling me about the heated guest cabin and the other amenities on your boat."

"Ah, yes." His mood visibly lightened. "We also have a snack bar and his-and-her restrooms. You'll also notice the large viewing windows as we pass through the galley on the way to the covered seating on the upper deck."

"It truly is a beautiful boat," Abby agreed, running her hand along the polished wood rail that encircled the exterior of the pilothouse.

"And one of the smoothest riding vessels that you'll ever experience. As you'll soon find out for yourself." He glanced at his pocket watch. "We'll be underway any minute now."

"I hope I can find a good spot," Abby told him as they left the engine room and returned to the top deck.

He smiled. "That's already been taken care of. I've reserved the best seat on the boat for you."

Abby was somewhat surprised by his generosity. It was almost as if he was trying to win her approval. But why? Perhaps to make up for his coolness toward her when they'd first met? If that was the case, the captain probably spent a lot of time making up for past behavior.

He led her to the front of the vessel where an empty deck chair awaited her directly behind the high glass windshield. "Here you go, Abby."

"This is wonderful," she exclaimed, setting her bag in the chair. "Thank you so much, Captain Hovel. I can't wait to get started."

"My pleasure," he replied with a short bow. "Now if you'll excuse me, I need to attend to a few details. But I'll check back to make certain that you have everything you need."

"I'm sure I'll be fine," she replied. "Please don't worry about me."

He smiled. "Enjoy the ride, Abby."

She watched him walk away, seeing more than one head turn at his impressive figure. He wore a neatly pressed navy blue uniform with brass buttons and a white cap with a captain's insignia embroidered in gold thread. No one could mistake the man in charge of this boat.

The engines grew louder as the boat began to slowly pull away from the marina.

"This is so exciting," said a woman seated next to Abby.

She looked about forty, with wide-set green eyes and tightly permed brown hair. "I've never been whale-watching before. To tell the truth, I've been on a boat only one time in my life and that's not counting the ferry that brought us to San Juan Island."

Abby couldn't imagine not growing up on the water, even as she realized everyone had their own special experiences. That's what made life so wondrous and fascinating.

"Where are you from?" Abby asked her.

"St. Louis, Missouri. My name is Glenda Middleton."

"Hi, Glenda," Abby said, shaking her hand. "I'm Abby Stanton. I live on Sparrow Island."

"Lucky you," Glenda replied. "We're here on vacation and when I read about that poor baby orca I had to book a whale-watching tour."

Glenda picked up the binoculars around her neck. "Do you think we might spot Poppy today?"

"That would be wonderful," Abby replied, knowing the chances were very slim. Still, just the fact that so many people would be looking for some sign of Poppy was heartwarming.

"It would be wonderful, wouldn't it?" Glenda breathed a wistful sigh. "If nothing else, I hope I get a chance to see Lulu."

"Lulu?" Abby echoed.

"She's the orca I adopted yesterday at The Whale Museum. They have an adoption program that lets people adopt an orca from one of the pods. Lulu is from the L pod."

Abby had heard about the adoption program and even considered doing something similar at the conservatory. "How will you be able to recognize Lulu?"

Glenda smiled. "The people at The Whale Museum told me they give each orca a number and a name after identifying it by the saddle patch and the shape and size of the dorsal fin. They even gave me a picture of Lulu, though I'm not sure I'll be able to tell her apart from the other orcas."

Abby knew a saddle patch was the gray and white markings beneath and behind the dorsal fin. "It sounds like a wonderful program."

The woman nodded. "The money goes to support orca research. I'm attending a regional nurses' conference when I get back home, so I'm planning to make an announcement about it there. Hopefully, my fellow nurses will adopt enough orcas to make a real difference."

Abby couldn't deny that Mick's publicity campaign would bring both money and attention to the San Juan Islands. Maybe Hugo had the right idea about hiring him to conduct public relations for the conservatory. The Whale Museum was no doubt benefiting from the funds generated by the interest in the orca adoption program.

The woman turned away as the man next to her began to ask questions about Lulu, giving Abby a chance to observe the other tourists around her. There were people of all ages and races, including several children who were gazing out on the water with expressions of awe on their innocent faces.

As the boat picked up speed, a feeling of exhilaration shot through Abby. It was a feeling she remembered from her own childhood when she used to accompany her father on his charter boat.

She'd always loved riding on the open water, a sensation that was as akin to flying as she could imagine. Abby used to stand on the deck of her father's boat, her arms stretched out at her sides so that her unzipped nylon jacket bubbled up behind her. The wind resistance had buoyed her up on her toes like a bird in flight.

Abby missed those days of perfect innocence. Yet, she couldn't regret the wisdom that came with age, either. It made her appreciate life so much more.

As the boat sailed over the beautiful blue water, Abby was reminded of one of her favorite Bible verses from the scriptural passage about the woman at the well.

"Jesus answered, 'Everyone who drinks this water will be thirsty again, but whoever drinks the water I give him will never thirst. Indeed, the water I give him will become in him a spring of water welling up to eternal life'" (John 4:13–14).

She was surrounded by water now, deeper and wider than she could even begin to imagine, but it was the water of life that fulfilled and sustained her.

One hour later, they sighted their first orca. Abby's breath caught in her throat as an adult orca breached the surface of the water, sending a spray of tiny droplets over the boat.

"I hope you're enjoying the tour, Abby."

Abby put down her binoculars, then turned around to see Captain Hovel standing behind her deck chair. "It's incredible."

Hovel gazed out at the orcas. "They are magnificent creatures."

"It's been so long since I've been whale-watching that I started to wonder if a boat could sail through the K pod without realizing it, but now I see that's impossible."

He nodded. "Yes, although the weather conditions are

perfect today, I suppose if it was dark or raining, it might be more difficult to get your bearings."

"Maybe," she mused, a thought tickling the back of her mind. "There was a storm that night, wasn't there?"

"What?" he asked, distracted by one of his sailors.

"There was a thunderstorm the night the mother orca was injured."

But Captain Hovel wasn't listening. The sailor had moved closer, his gestures becoming frantic now.

"What's the matter, Jones?" Captain Hovel barked. "Why aren't you at your station?"

"It's *The Sea Prince*, sir," Jones sputtered, pointing to a boat in the distance. "She's in trouble!"

Fear clutched Abby deep inside as she lifted her binoculars to her eyes. *The Sea Prince* now belonged to Kyle Breslin.

"What kind of trouble?" Captain Hovel demanded as the passengers around them began to take notice of the agitated sailor.

"I just saw the signal myself, sir," Jones replied, his eyes wide with horror. "*The Sea Prince* is sinking!"

CHAPTER ✤ THIRTEEN

Captain Hovel strode up to Jones. "Get hold of yourself and tell me what you saw."

The sailor gulped, then sucked in a deep breath. "I was on the starboard side, pointing out an orca to one of the passengers. I saw a flash in the distance and saw a tour boat. Then I saw another flash and realized they were signaling us."

"You're sure about that?" Hovel demanded.

"Positive, sir," the sailor replied. "It was an SOS signal. Their radio must be down."

That was all Captain Hovel needed to hear. He bounded to the engine room, shouting orders at his crew. *The Adventurer* backed slowly away from the K pod, then with a roar of its engines, turned around and sped in the direction of the foundering *Sea Prince.*

Abby gripped the railing, her heart caught in her throat as she silently prayed that they would reach the tour boat in time. Grabbing her binoculars, she adjusted the lenses until *The Sea Prince* came into view. It was tipped in the water at a frightening angle, all the passengers gathered on the high side of the deck.

If we don't get there in time . . .

Abby knew all the whale-watch tour boats were equipped with inflatable rafts and life preservers, but she hoped they didn't need to use them. Panicked passengers could overload a raft and cause it to overturn. She didn't even want to think about people in the cold water.

"Heavenly Father," she prayed aloud, "please protect the passengers of *The Sea Prince* and uphold them during this difficult and scary time. Give us strength to be of service to them."

"Amen," said Glenda, standing beside her. She grabbed Abby's hand, giving it a warm squeeze. "They'll be all right, won't they?"

She heard the worry in the woman's voice and wished she could reassure her. But unlike Glenda, Abby's long history on the water told her this was a very dangerous situation. "I hope so."

As *The Adventurer* neared *The Sea Prince*, Abby began to hear the frightened cries of the passengers on the sinking vessel.

"Help us!" a man shouted into the wind. "Please, God, help us."

Abby's grip tightened on the railing. She'd never felt so helpless.

"'In my distress,'" Glenda quoted softly, "'I called to the Lord; I called out to my God. From his temple he heard my voice; my cry came to his ears'" (2 Samuel 22:7).

The words comforted Abby and propelled her into action. She needed to let God work through her and the other people on *The Adventurer*.

"We have to get organized," Abby told Glenda. "This is a rescue operation. We'll have to find towels and blankets. Also, any medical supplies that are on board."

"There may be other nurses on deck," Glenda said. "As well as EMTs or paramedics. I'll try to round them all up."

Abby turned to face the passengers on the upper deck. "We'll probably be taking on passengers from *The Sea Prince*," she called out to them. "Some of them may be hurt or ill. We need to set up an area to care for them."

Several of the men volunteered to take on that job. A group of the women on board began gathering jackets and blankets and bandages. Other people began to stockpile their food, water and other emergency supplies in a central location.

Captain Hovel's deep voice came over the public address system as he hailed *The Sea Prince*.

"Ahoy," he shouted as *The Adventurer* sailed closer to the sinking boat. "Ahoy, there! We're here to help you. Please stay calm."

Abby saw Captain Kyle Breslin shouting orders to his harried crew. When he heard Captain Hovel hailing him, he ran over to the bow of his ship, holding a bullhorn in his hand.

"My radio is out," Kyle shouted, his voice amplified through the bull horn. "My boat is taking on water and I don't know how much longer we can stay afloat. I have fifty passengers aboard and six crewmen. Can you take them all? "

Abby held her breath, uncertain of the carrying capacity of *The Adventurer*. If Hovel denied the request, she feared the passengers on *The Sea Prince* might start jumping overboard to reach the safety of *The Adventurer*.

"Affirmative," Captain Hovel responded. "We will transfer the children and elderly first. I've already contacted the Coast Guard and they're on the way."

Glenda approached Abby. "I found one other nurse and two qualified EMTs. Where do you want us?"

Abby pointed toward the heated guest cabin. "We've got a triage area set up there for passengers with any injuries."

"Good," Glenda replied. "There may be some people in shock or having chest pains. That's not unusual in these situations, especially for the elderly."

They both watched in silence as Captain Hovel performed the difficult task of carefully steering *The Adventurer* until it came up flush against the side of the listing *The Sea Prince*.

Abby winced at the sound of steel scraping against steel until *The Adventurer* came to a full stop.

The passengers of *The Sea Prince* rushed toward the railing, eager to abandon the sinking ship.

"Children and elderly first," Captain Hovel commanded over the public address system. "We have room for all. I repeat, we have room for all."

Abby watched the young Captain Breslin restore order on his boat, organizing the passengers in groups of the most vulnerable to the least. Then some of the stronger males on board *The Sea Prince* assisted his crew in transferring each passenger across the rails and into the waiting arms of sailors aboard *The Adventurer*.

Abby found herself silently praying for God's help and guidance even as she began assisting the oncoming passengers. Her experience with search-and-rescue missions automatically kicked in.

As each frightened child came aboard, Abby assigned an adult to watch over the child until their parent or guardian could be located. As the elderly passengers began to arrive, several of them complained of chest pains or palpitations. Abby immediately sent them to Glenda's triage area for care.

She also assigned someone to keep a count of all the

passengers that came aboard. That was the quickest way to become aware of any missing passengers once they reached the shore.

As the last elderly woman was carried over to *The Adventurer*, Abby took a moment to appreciate the way the passengers had all pulled together to help one another. She realized she was witnessing one of God's miracles and held it in her heart.

As some of the younger passengers were transferred onto *The Adventurer*, the Coast Guard arrived, allowing everyone to breathe a collective sigh of relief.

The Coast Guard officers started assisting with the rescue operation, helping the remaining passengers on *The Sea Prince* onto the Coast Guard vessels.

"Abby!"

She turned at the sound of her name and saw Ana Dominquez hurrying toward her.

"Ana, are you all right?" Abby asked, surprised to see the woman here.

Ana and her husband Juan lived in Green Harbor, where he worked as a nurse at the hospital and she owned In Stitches, a handcraft store filled with her beautiful fiber creations.

"I brought my grandson Mateo to see the orcas," Ana explained, the soft lilt of a Spanish accent in her trembling voice. "He's been hearing all about that missing orca calf and wanted to visit his *abuela* so he could look for her."

"You two were on *The Sea Prince*?"

"*Sí.* If only we'd taken *The Sea Star* instead."

The Sea Star was a whale-watching tour boat that operated out of Sparrow Island. It was owned by Warren Meyers, a member of Abby's church. She hadn't ever considered him a suspect in the orca incident, since *The Sea Star* usually ran a route that followed the J pod, not the K pod.

Ana clutched Abby's hands in her own. "Now I've lost track of my Mateo. He's only five. I'm so worried."

Abby's heart went out to the woman, knowing how frantic she must be. Ana's face was pale and her hands were ice cold, making Abby worry about her.

"Are you sure you're all right?" Abby asked her. "Would you like to see a nurse?"

"No, no," Ana assured her. "I'm fine. I just need to find Mateo."

Abby gave her a warm hug. "Don't worry, Ana. I'll help you look for him."

They wove around the upper deck, searching for Ana's five-year-old grandson. The deck was crowded with people, many of them half-covered by jackets and blankets.

"What does Mateo look like?" Abby asked her.

Ana rubbed a hand over her pale cheeks. "He has dark hair and the most beautiful brown eyes. And a small scar," she pointed above her left eyebrow, "right about here. He got it playing soccer with his sister."

Abby didn't see any child matching that description on the lower deck. "Let's go look on the upper deck," she said, taking Ana by the hand and heading for the stairs.

When they reached the upper deck, she headed over to Glenda's triage station. "I'm helping Ana search for her grandson, Mateo Dominquez. He's five years old and has dark hair and eyes. Have you seen him?"

Glenda thought for a moment, then shook her head. "I'm sorry, I don't think I have."

"Ana's very worried about him," Abby said, watching the woman wobble a little bit on her feet.

Glenda hurried over to help support her. "I'm sure your grandson's fine. Why don't you sit down here for just a moment to catch your breath."

"All right," Ana agreed, her voice thin and weary.

As Glenda led Ana to a chair, she gently placed her fingers around her wrist to take her pulse. Then she looked back at Abby and gave her a reassuring nod.

"I'll keep looking for Mateo," Abby told Ana. "You wait right here for me until I get back."

"Thank you, Abby," Ana said, sagging into the deck chair.

Abby walked along the upper deck where most of the children had been taken after leaving *The Sea Prince* to make room for more incoming passengers.

Some of the children were chattering like magpies, still caught up in the excitement of their ordeal. Others cried softly and shrank from the strangers around them. As more adults came aboard *The Adventurer*, there were cries of happiness and relief when a child was reunited with his or her parent.

As Abby looked around, she began to fear that Mateo hadn't made it onto *The Adventurer*. She hoped he hadn't gotten scared and hidden himself somewhere on *The Sea Prince*. She was about to go to Captain Hovel to tell him about the missing child when she saw a dark head pop out from under a blanket.

"Peek-a-boo!" he exclaimed to the woman sitting next to him.

"Mateo?" Abby called out.

He whirled around at the sound of his name. "I'm Mateo."

Abby almost jumped with relief. She walked over to him

and knelt down beside his chair. "I'm so glad I found you, Mateo. My name's Abby."

"Hi, Abby," he said with a grin.

Abby looked up at the woman who had been assigned to watch over Mateo. "His grandmother is in the triage area. She asked me to take Mateo there when I found him."

"Go right ahead," the woman replied, affectionately ruffling the hair on the little boy's head. "But I'm going to miss this cutie."

Mateo reached for Abby's hand. "I want my grandma."

"All right, Mateo," Abby said, "let's go find her."

As he slipped the blanket off his shoulders and hopped off the deck chair, his guardian said, "Bye, Mateo."

He turned to wave to her. "Bye, Mrs. Hogan."

Ana saw them approaching the triage area. "Mateo!"

"Grandma," he cried, releasing Abby's hand and running into the outstretched arms of his grandmother.

Ana scooped him up, hugging him tightly against her plump body. "*Gracias,* Lord," she cried, tears gleaming in her eyes. "*Gracias.*"

Abby's heart warmed at the touching reunion. She exchanged glances with Glenda, grateful to have had her capable help and prayers during this ordeal.

"Are you all right, mijo?" Ana asked her grandson.

"I'm great," Mateo replied. "I got a chocolate chip cookie and some juice from Mrs. Hogan. Then we played games."

Ana beamed up at Abby. "I'll have to thank this Mrs. Hogan for taking such good care of my grandson."

The jet engines began to stir and Abby looked up to see that the evacuation of *The Sea Prince* was complete. Captain Breslin stood aboard one of the Coast Guard vessels, talking intently to members of his crew.

"Ladies and gentleman," announced Captain Hovel over the public address system. "We will now return to the Friday Harbor marina. We are slightly above the boat's capacity, so the ride back will be slower than before. I ask that you please be patient. All passengers aboard *The Adventurer* will be fully reimbursed for this tour."

Abby helped keep some of the children occupied on the long, slow trip back by telling colorful stories of different birds that she had rehabilitated.

When *The Adventurer* finally docked, a sense of calm washed over her. God had answered all of their prayers for a safe return.

Captain Hovel sought her out after the passengers had disembarked. "Thank you, Abby. I don't know how we would have done it without your help."

"You're welcome," Abby replied. "You did a wonderful job of creating a calm atmosphere. I'm just so relieved that everyone's safe."

"As am I." He glanced over at Kyle, who stood on the dock giving a report to a Coast Guard officer. "I just can't imagine why Breslin would take a ship out that wasn't seaworthy."

"Is that what happened?" Abby asked, surprised that the cause of the problem had already been determined.

"I can't say for certain," he replied with a shrug of his shoulders. "At the very least, he should have had *The Sea Prince* inspected before he bought it. It's well known around here that the owner of North Star Cruises likes to cut corners. Looks like this time he'll pay for it."

It was hard to imagine that the Kyle she'd met, so friendly and open, could be indifferent to the safety of his passengers. Yet, she remembered thinking that he'd said he wanted to be a ruthless businessman like his father.

Did Kyle really cut corners to save a few pennies at the expense of his passengers? Or was that just speculation on the part of Captain Hovel?

"I'm sorry your tour to see the orcas was cut short," Captain Hovel said. "I hope you'll let me give you a raincheck."

Before she could reply, a Coast Guard officer called Captain Hovel away to question him about the incident.

Abby helped some of the frazzled passengers arrange transportation back to their hotels, then joined Ana and Mateo on the ferry back to Sparrow Island.

When they arrived in Green Harbor, a very worried Juan Dominquez was waiting for them on the dock. He ran up to Ana and Mateo as they disembarked, throwing his arms around them both.

Ana hugged her husband, then spoke quickly in Spanish, her words making him turn to Abby.

"Thank you, Abby," he said, his voice tight with emotion, "for taking care of my wife and grandson."

"I didn't really do that much," Abby said, embarrassed by the accolades she was receiving.

"You were a good friend," Ana countered. "That's the best kind of help there is."

Abby reached out to hug her. "I'm just glad you and Mateo are safe."

She watched the Dominquez family leave the dock, then took a deep breath and looked around to see if anyone else needed any assistance. Most of *The Sea Prince* passengers who had taken the ferry to Sparrow Island were now being greeted by family and friends, the news of the incident having spread rather quickly.

As she turned to leave, she saw her father racing toward her across the dock. He had the same expression she'd seen on his face in the hospital after Mary's car accident.

"Abby," George cried when he reached her. "Are you all right?"

"I'm fine, Dad," Abby said, though she felt a little shaky now that it was all over.

"Barney called me as soon as he heard the news," George explained. "But he wasn't sure which ship was in trouble, *The Sea Prince* or *The Adventurer*. I got here as fast as I could."

"I was on *The Adventurer*," she clarified, lightly patting his arm. "It was *The Sea Prince* that was in trouble. I was never in any danger."

He pulled her into a hug, holding her tight. "Thank you, God, for watching over my little girl."

She laid her head on her father's shoulder and hugged him back. Abby was a fifty-five-year-old professional woman, but she knew in that moment that no matter what her age, she would always be George Stanton's little girl.

CHAPTER ❧ FOURTEEN

O N   F R I D A Y   M O R N I N G, Abby left early for the conservatory, eager to get away from Mary's fussing over her. While she appreciated the concern of her big sister and her parents, Abby herself had never been in danger aboard *The Adventurer*.

She knew her parents' attention stemmed from the memory of Mary's accident and how close they had come to losing her. It reminded Abby how precious her family was to her, and she had said a special prayer for each one of them during her morning devotional.

The Sea Prince had been on her mind ever since she'd left Friday Harbor. She couldn't help but wonder if the near disaster might somehow be connected to the orca pod incident. There were too many strange occurrences happening with the whale-watch tour boats to be a coincidence.

First, *The Luna* had been vandalized, then *The Sea Prince* was suddenly sold and her captain pulled a disappearing act. Dennis Zirka still hadn't made an appearance or contacted anyone about his whereabouts. Then Kyle Breslin captains *The Sea Prince* on a tour and it starts to go down.

If Abby didn't know better, she'd think someone was deliberately trying to throw her off track in her search for the boat that had sailed through the orca pod. There were too many suspects. Too many motives.

Which made her wonder what piece of the puzzle she was missing.

For now, all she could do was wait for the results of *The Sea Prince* investigation. In the meantime, she was going to turn her attention back to her duties at the conservatory.

The day had dawned clear and bright, perfect for sending Homer back to his home, wherever that might be. She just hoped the message she was sending back with him would get there in time.

Bobby met her at the small set of cages outside the conservatory where she had set up Homer two days ago. She'd wanted him to get acclimated to the outdoors again before he set off on his flight home.

"I think he knows something special is happening today," Bobby told her. "He's been cooing at me all morning."

Abby believed birds could sense moods, much like they could sense changes in the weather. Perhaps Homer sensed he was going home today. He certainly seemed strong enough now, hopping around in his cage and climbing up the sides.

"I think we're just about ready," Abby said, slipping her bag off of her shoulder.

"Don't forget the message," Bobby reminded her as he carefully opened Homer's cage.

Abby hadn't forgotten. She pulled the message, along with

the yellow tube that would be attached to Homer's leg, out of her bag. She read their message aloud one more time, just to make certain she hadn't forgotten anything.

"My name is Abby Stanton. Your pigeon was injured and unable to continue its journey. Please contact me at the Sparrow Island Nature Conservatory in the San Juan Islands for more information."

Bobby pursed his lips. "Are you sure we shouldn't send the message in code? What if it falls into the wrong hands?"

She smiled at his concern. "I don't think that's going to happen. Besides, I'm going to include the coded message that was in the tube before so they'll know it wasn't delivered."

"I hope somebody does contact you," Bobby said wistfully. "That would be so cool to see where Homer came from and how far he flew."

"That *would* be cool," Abby agreed. She rolled up both of the messages into a tight scroll, then slipped them in the tube before capping it. "I think we're ready."

"Are you ready, Homer?" Bobby asked him, gently stroking the top of the pigeon's head. The bird replied with tiny coos as he nuzzled against Bobby's long fingers.

"Is that a yes?" Abby asked him.

Bobby nodded, though he didn't look as enthusiastic as before. "I'm really going to miss him."

"I know you are," Abby said softly. "You've been a good friend to Homer. I think you're a big part of the reason that he recovered from his injury so quickly."

Bobby looked up at her, affection for Homer shining in his eyes. "Really?"

"Really," Abby affirmed. She pulled her digital camera out

of her birding vest. "How about a picture of the two of you before we let Homer go?"

Bobby's face brightened at the idea. "Okay."

She waited until Bobby held up Homer next to his face to pose for the camera, then snapped the picture.

Bobby raced over to catch the image on the display screen. "Hey, that's a good one."

"It is," Abby agreed. "I'll print out a copy for you later today."

Bobby turned back to the pigeon. "Well, I guess it's time to say good-bye, Homer."

The pigeon cooed at him, pecking him lightly on the tip of his nose.

Bobby handed the pigeon over to Abby, then helped her attach the yellow tube to the pigeon's leg. They made sure it wasn't too tight or too loose so it wouldn't interfere with Homer's flight.

"Bon Voyage, Homer," Abby said, a lump in her throat. She'd miss the pigeon, too. She always felt a close attachment to the birds that she rehabilitated, but Homer was special. Most of the birds she cared for were wild and anxious to be on their own again. Homer was more like a pet and had found his way into her heart.

"Don't stop to play with other birds on the way home," Bobby admonished the bird. "And make sure you get plenty to eat and drink on the trip."

Abby didn't want to think about what might happen if Homer encountered another storm and was injured again. The Bible warned about the futility of worry, though often that admonition was easy to forget. Abby needed to put her faith in God to keep watch over the earth and everything in it.

She handed the pigeon back to Bobby. "Here, I'll let you do the honors."

Bobby dropped a light kiss on the top of Homer's head, then threw his arms up to release the pigeon into the air. Homer sailed high above their heads, flapping his wings to lift himself toward the sky.

"Look at him go!" Bobby squinted into the morning sun.

Abby smiled as the pigeon climbed higher and higher, circling them overhead. There was no doubt that Homer's wing had fully recovered from the injury. He looked strong and healthy.

The pigeon circled above them again, seeming in no hurry to be on his way. Abby shaded her eyes from the sun as she watched him.

"I think he's confused," Bobby said, as the pigeon circled the observatory for a third time.

Abby didn't know what to think. Homer showed no signs of physical impairment, illness or lethargy. Yet, he also showed no signs of wanting to leave.

They watched him circle a few more times, then he descended from the sky and landed on the top of Bobby's head.

"Hey, Homer," Bobby said, tenderly lifting the bird off his hair. "What's going on with you?"

Homer cooed in response.

"He must not be ready to go," Abby said with a sigh of disappointment.

"But he's flying great."

"I know," Abby said, "but maybe he's not quite strong enough for the long flight yet. We need to trust his instincts. Homer will let us know when he's ready to go home."

Bobby nodded, then looked up at her with a grin. "Does this mean he gets to stay with us for a little while longer?"

"It sure does."

"Yahoo!" Bobby shouted, twirling in circles with the bird in his hands.

She watched Bobby and Homer play together, a tangle of emotions inside of her. She was happy for Bobby that his feathered playmate wasn't leaving yet, but she couldn't help worrying about that undelivered message.

It might be too late already. Someone, somewhere, would be waiting for a meeting that would never take place.

THIRTY MINUTES LATER, Hugo Baron found Abby working inside her office where she was transcribing notes from her microcassette recorder onto her laptop.

"There you are," he said, pausing in the doorway. "Is this a bad time?"

"Not at all," she assured him. "I was just finishing up here."

Hugo walked inside her office. "We've been crossing paths these last few days, and I haven't had a chance to talk to you."

A warm glow flared inside of Abby. It was nice to be missed. "You know you can call me anytime if you need anything."

"Oh, I know," he said with a smile. "It was nothing urgent. I was just hoping for an update on this orca situation. Have you discovered anything yet?"

Abby wished she had better news for him. "Not much, I'm afraid. We're not any closer to finding Poppy, although the publicity has been tremendous."

Hugo nodded. "I know. Calls are coming in almost non-stop here. Unfortunately, most of them are asking questions about the missing Poppy instead of providing answers."

"I thought the calls might be tapering off by now," Abby mused.

He shook his head. "Mick's keeping the story alive in all the newspapers. It made the front page of this week's *Birdcall*."

Abby picked up a copy from the top of her desk. She hadn't had a chance to read it yet and was surprised to see the bold headline.

"Authorities Closing in on Suspect in Orca Case," she read aloud. She leaned back in her chair as she read the rest of the article.

"In an exclusive interview with marine biologist Mick Wymore, *The Birdcall* has learned that the person suspected of injuring the mother orca and disrupting the K pod will soon be apprehended."

She paused to look at Hugo. "What suspect?"

"Keep reading," he replied.

"While Wymore refused to reveal the name of the suspect," she continued, "he did say that evidence was mounting and that a conviction of a local tour boat operator was likely in the case. Wymore also said he expects it to be resolved within the next few days. Unfortunately, there are no further developments in the search for the missing orca calf named Poppy who disappeared when her mother Rosie was injured."

She looked up at Hugo. "Where did Mick get the information for this article?"

"That's what I was hoping you could tell me."

"I have no idea," she said. "I haven't heard about any of this from Henry and I've talked to all of the whale-watch tour boat captains, except Dennis Zirka. He seems to have disappeared."

Hugo rubbed his chin. "Mick made it clear in the article

that he believes it's one of the tour boat captains. But which one?"

Abby thought about it, going over each suspect in her mind. "*The Luna* seems the most likely culprit, considering the damage done to the hull. The Andersons had a motive, too."

"The insurance money?" Hugo ventured.

She nodded. "But I just can't believe they would do something like this. Maybe I'm biased because they're friends with my parents."

Hugo sat down across from her. "You've talked to the Andersons?"

"Yes," she replied. "They're good people. I know that won't stand up in a court of law, but I just can't see them sailing through the K pod with no concern for the orcas."

"I can't either," he agreed. "But you're right as far as physical evidence. The boat that collided with the mother orca had to sustain some kind of damage. What about the other tour boats?"

"*The Adventurer* looks fine to me," Abby conceded. "I sailed on it yesterday."

"Yes," Hugo replied, his blue eyes softening, "I heard about your heroics. I'm so glad you were there to help."

"I was hardly heroic," she said humbly. "Just helping out in any way that I could. I have to say I was impressed with Captain Hovel's handling of the situation, even though . . ."

Her voice trailed off as Abby found herself unable to put her feelings into words.

"Even though?" Hugo prodded.

"I can't put my finger on it," she continued. "There's something about Captain Hovel that bothers me. It's almost as if he's two different people."

"How so?"

"It's the way he treats his crew," she said at last. "He's short-tempered with them, and it's easy to tell they're not too fond of him, either."

"Some people would say that's the kind of man you need to run a tight ship," Hugo countered.

"I suppose so." Abby's mind drifted to the incident yesterday and another thought hit her. "I wonder if *The Sea Prince* started sinking because of damage to the underside of her hull. Is it possible *The Sea Prince* collided with Rosie and it took this long for the consequences of the impact to show?"

Hugo considered that scenario. "I suppose it could be like having a slow leak in a tire on a car. A little leak that gradually grows bigger and bigger until you can't help but notice it."

"We should find something out soon if that's the case." Abby placed the newspaper back on her desk. "According to Mary, Henry's part of the investigative team since they suspect foul play. *The Sea Prince* was able to be towed back to shore before it sank so we'll soon know what caused it to founder."

Hugo's brow furrowed. "Captain Breslin just bought *The Sea Prince*, didn't he?"

Abby nodded. "Yes, from Captain Zirka, who has mysteriously disappeared. Oh, and there's a sailor named Judd Peavey who used to work on *The Sea Prince*. Apparently he knows something about the boat that sailed through the K pod, but he's refusing to talk about it."

Hugo's eyes widened at the news. "What? There's a witness? This Judd fellow has got to tell the authorities what he knows."

"I agree," Abby replied, "but when I questioned him about it, Judd completely clammed up. He's not talking. I don't know if it's because of some distorted sense of loyalty or maybe even fear."

"Perhaps if I try to talk to him," Hugo suggested.

Abby shook her head. "I don't think it would do any good, Hugo, but thank you for offering. I have an old friend at the marina, Barney Magee, who's working on him. If anyone can get Judd to come forward with the information, Barney can."

Hugo stood up and reached for the newspaper on Abby's desk. "What I don't understand is who Mick believes is the suspect. Unless he knows something that we don't. He certainly seems to have made a lot of contacts in the short amount of time that he's been here."

Abby found herself just as curious. "I'm having lunch with him today, so hopefully I'll find out what he knows."

If he knows anything, Abby thought to herself. Something told her that Mick wouldn't be averse to stretching the truth, though she didn't have anything to base it on. Just that he was young and brash and seemed to be caught up in all the hype of the moment.

When Hugo left her office, Abby picked up the telephone and dialed her old friend at Cornell, Dr. Lauren Sima.

"Hello?" answered a voice on the other end of the line that Abby didn't recognize.

"May I speak to Dr. Sima, please?"

"I'm sorry, she isn't here right now," replied the girl. "May I take a message?"

Abby suppressed a sigh of disappointment, not surprised that she'd missed her friend. Even when Abby had worked at Cornell, Lauren had never been easy to catch. She was so involved with her classes and various university organizations that she was always on the move. "This is Dr. Abby Stanton. Will you please ask Dr. Sima to call me at her convenience?"

"Dr. Stanton?" the girl cried in surprise. "Wow, this is a surprise! I'm Kayla Winston. I took your Intro to Ornithology class here a few years ago. You probably don't remember me."

"Hello, Kayla," Abby said, trying to place a face with the name and not having much success. That particular lecture class usually had over a hundred students registered for it each semester. "How are you?"

"I'm great," Kayla replied. "I'm a grad student now working under Dr. Sima. She's awesome."

Abby smiled. There was no better compliment for a college professor. "I think so, too. There's another student of hers here in the San Juan Islands with me now. His name is Mick Wymore."

"Mick!" she squealed. "Oh wow, I don't believe it. I wondered what had happened to him."

"So you know Mick?" Abby asked in surprise.

"Well, not as well as I'd like to," Kayla quipped. "He's such a hunk. That guy's going to be famous some day, just mark my words. Another Jacques Cousteau."

Abby was impressed that Kayla even knew the name Jacques Cousteau, much less that he was famous. "Mick does seem very nice."

"Oh, he's awesome," Kayla affirmed. "Really, really awesome."

Her unadulterated adoration of Mick made Abby feel better about making the phone call to check up on him. "I'll tell him you said so, Kayla. We're having lunch this afternoon."

"Lucky you," Kayla replied. "Just tell him crazy Kayla said hello. He'll know who you mean."

"I'll do that," Abby promised. "Please tell Dr. Sima that I called."

"Gotcha," Kayla said, then rang off.

Abby hung up the phone, adding another name to Mick Wymore's fan club. If she was smart, Abby would get his autograph at lunch just in case he ever did become as famous as Jacques Cousteau.

CHAPTER ❦ FIFTEEN

I LOVE THIS PLACE," MICK said as he opened the menu in front of him. "It's so quaint and I've heard that the food here is great."

They sat at a table in the Springhouse Café, near the window that looked out onto Randolph Bay. Abby was glad they'd arrived before the noon rush because the restaurant was filling up fast.

"The food is wonderful," Abby said, glancing at her menu. "I think I'm going to have the special today. How about you?"

"Sounds good," he replied as their waitress approached.

Ida Tolliver, wearing the café uniform of blue khakis and a white top, donned a wide smile when she saw Abby seated in her section. "Hello, there. This is a nice surprise."

"Hello, Ida," Abby replied. "I'd like you to meet a friend of mine. This is Mick Wymore. Mick, this is Ida Tolliver."

"Nice to meet you," Mick said, rising to his feet and extending his hand.

Ida's eyes widened when she heard his name. "I know you.

You're the guy who's been on television and in the newspapers about the missing orca calf."

He smiled. "That's right. I'm just trying to help out any way I can."

"I think it's absolutely wonderful." Ida flipped her blonde hair over her thin shoulder. "I've heard you've traveled all around the world and been to so many fabulous places. I never imagined I'd find you sitting at my table."

Mick laughed. "I'm thrilled to be here."

Ida stared at him a moment longer, then seemed to catch herself. "Oh, you two probably want to order some lunch."

"I'll have the crab cake special and a glass of iced tea," Abby told her.

"Make it the same for me," Mick added.

Ida jotted down their orders, took their menus, then flashed a shy smile at Mick before turning around and heading toward the kitchen.

"She seems nice," Mick said folding his hands together on the table.

"Ida's great," Abby replied, thinking of how much the young woman had grown in the time she'd known her.

Ida attended Little Flock now and her spiritual journey had helped Abby renew and strengthen her own faith. At twenty-four, Ida was taking some college classes, too, committed to improving herself.

"I don't think I've ever met nicer people than here on Sparrow Island," Mick mused. "So friendly and helpful. I'm not sure I'll ever want to leave."

She thought about Hugo's interest in hiring Mick as a publicist for the conservatory and realized he might never have to leave if he took the job. He certainly seemed popular in the short time he'd been here, especially with the young ladies.

"So what have you been up to lately?" Mick asked her, taking a sip of the ice water in front of him.

"I've been rehabilitating a homing pigeon," Abby replied, "and raising up a trio of double-crested cormorant chicks. That, along with investigating the orca pod disturbance, has kept me quite busy."

He nodded, impressed. "Any progress in the investigation?"

"I think I should be asking you that question." Abby curled her palms around her glass. "It sounds like you're one step ahead of me."

His brow crinkled. "What do you mean?"

"I saw the article in *The Birdcall* where you announced a prime suspect in the case."

He grinned. "Got your attention, didn't it?"

"It sure did." Abby paused as Ida brought their salad plates to the table.

"I threw on some extra croutons for you," Ida said, her violet eyes fixed on Mick. "This place is swamped, but let me know if you need anything. Those specials should be out soon."

"We will," Abby promised.

"Catch you later," Mick said with a wink.

Ida giggled, then backed away from their table, almost running into another waitress carrying a large tray full of water glasses.

"That was a close one," Mick observed, turning back to Abby. "Now where were we?"

"You were just about to tell me about the prime suspect in the orca case." Abby placed the napkin across her lap. "The one you said the authorities are closing in on."

"Wasn't that a great line?" he said. "Of course, I was bluffing."

She blinked in surprise. "Bluffing?"

"Sure." Mick picked up his fork and started digging into his salad. "I just threw out some bait. Now we've just got to sit back and hope the culprit takes it so we can reel him in."

"You mean you lied in the article?"

He shrugged. "If you want to call it that. One of my friends is a cop back in New York. He said police use deception all the time to catch the bad guys. So I decided to turn up the heat a little bit. Make the culprit nervous. Maybe even nervous enough to slip up and make him easier to catch."

"What about William?" she asked.

His brow furrowed in confusion. "William who?"

"William Jansen," she clarified, "the editor of *The Birdcall.* Was he in on this trick, too?"

"No." Mick looked at her, chewing thoughtfully. Then he said, "I get the feeling you're not too thrilled about the article, Abby. Should I have told him we're no closer to catching the person who hurt Rosie than we were the day it happened?"

Abby didn't know what to think. Maybe Mick was right and police did lie all the time. She'd have to ask Henry about it. On the other hand, the Bible was clear about lying and it never listed exceptions, even for a good cause.

Ida arrived with their crab cakes, curtailing the conversation. "Here you go," she said, setting a plate in front of each of them. "May I get you anything else?"

Abby glanced at Mick, then shook her head. "I think this will do it."

The distinctive chime of a cell phone sounded from Mick's jacket. He plucked it out of his pocket as he rose to his feet. "I need to take this call. Will you please excuse me for a moment?"

"Of course," Abby told him.

When he walked away, Ida sat down in his empty chair. "Mick Wymore's the most magnificent man I've ever seen. I mean, what a hunk! Don't you think he's adorable?"

Abby laughed. "He's certainly seems to be forming quite a fan club around here."

"And with very good reason." Ida feigned fanning herself with her hand. "He looks like a movie star, plus he seems super nice and very polite. What more could a girl want?"

Ida hadn't always had the best luck with men. Abby couldn't help thinking that she didn't even know Mick, other than his appearances on local television and in the newspapers. The waitress did have an ongoing flirtation with Aaron Holloway, a very nice young man who was still looking for direction in his life. No doubt a man with Mick's credentials probably seemed more stable to her.

"She could want values and integrity," Abby said with a gentle smile. "A man she can share her life with as well as her faith."

"Oh, I know all that," Ida said with a sigh. "But that kind of man seems to be a lot harder to find. Not that I'm ready to give up looking just yet."

"I'm not saying that Mick doesn't have those qualities," Abby told her. "I don't really know him well enough to say either way."

"Hopefully, I will know him well enough if he sticks around Sparrow Island," Ida said, then hopped out of the chair when she saw Mick returning to the table. "I'd better get back to work. Let me know if you need anything."

Mick sat down at the table, watching Ida scurry away. "I hope I didn't scare her off."

"I don't think there's any danger of that," Abby mused as she picked up her fork.

"Sorry about that phone call." Mick's blue eyes flashed with excitement. "It was from my agent . . . well, the guy who might soon be my agent. There seems to be some interest in developing the orca story into a movie."

Abby almost dropped her fork. "Really?"

He nodded, leaning toward her. "It's got all the elements they look for in a good movie: injured mother orca; missing baby orca; a villain responsible for it all. The only thing they're still waiting for is the happy ending. So this is even more incentive for us to make sure it turns out well."

Abby had been hoping and praying for a happy ending from the beginning, but she didn't say anything to dampen Mick's enthusiasm. He was still young enough to be dazzled by the allure of fame and fortune. She'd learned in her fifty-five years that family and good friends were of far greater value.

Mick's cell phone rang again. He tossed her an apologetic smile as he pulled it out of his pocket. "I'm really sorry about this, Abby. Do you mind if I take this call?"

"Not at all."

Abby watched more than one head turn as Mick walked toward a secluded area in the restaurant to speak on the phone. The orca situation had brought him a lot of attention.

She just hoped he didn't let it go to his head.

THE FOLLOWING DAY, Abby headed for Kingfisher Avenue to talk to Ana Dominquez. Her shop, In Stitches, was directly across the street from The Tackle Shop. When she walked inside, she saw Ana talking to Henry Cobb. He wore his uniform so she figured he must be here on official police business.

Abby bided her time by browsing through Ana's shop. She enjoyed the opportunity to look at the new creations on the shelves. Though not as artistically talented as her sister, Abby enjoyed viewing all of the different crafts. The ones that intrigued her the most were the souvenirs Ana made from natural materials she found on the island.

A quartet of young girls were clustered in an aisle full of beads and thin leather strips used for making bracelets. Abby smiled to herself, remembering when she and Mary had made necklaces and bracelets out of wildflowers when they were the same age.

As she moved around the store, Abby came to an aisle full of woodcrafts. There were several small pieces of furniture, as well as bird and marine life carvings. She found jewelry, too, very similar to the tupelo wood brooch she'd purchased at that kiosk on the marina at Friday Harbor.

"Hello, Abby."

She looked up to see Henry walking toward her. "Hello, there."

"Doing a little shopping today?" he asked, perusing the shelves.

"That wasn't my intention when I came in here, but I'm not sure I'll be able to resist buying something. Ana has so many beautiful items to choose from."

The sound of Ana's laughter made them both look across the shop, where the owner was busy helping the little girls choose beads for their bracelets.

"I'm tempted to buy something for Mary myself," he said,

moving further into the aisle. "This caught my eye when I came into the store."

Abby watched him pick up a jewelry box, the carved lid was exquisitely stained to create the picture of an exotic bird surrounded by lush orchids.

"What do you think?" he asked her, running his fingers over the polished teak surface.

"I think she'll love it," Abby replied, touched by Henry's thoughtfulness in his choice. He knew Mary treasured her jewelry and the flowers on the top of the box reflected her gift with plants.

Henry tucked the jewelry box under his arm. "Then Ana just made a sale."

"Say, Henry," Abby said before he could leave. "Do you mind if I ask you a question?"

"Fire away."

She hesitated, hoping her query wouldn't offend him. "Do you ever lie when you're trying to catch a criminal?"

He pondered her words for a moment. "I know there are many police officers who do, especially during an interrogation. People are often very surprised to learn that the police are allowed to lie in order to make a suspect confess. Sometimes they lie about evidence they've collected or they'll claim that there's an eyewitness to the crime when there's really not."

"And that works?"

"Often, it does work," he told her. "But I've never been comfortable with lying to anyone, so I use another technique."

"Really? Do you mind sharing it with me?"

"It's simple," he replied. "I prefer to let people trap themselves. Most criminals, other than sociopaths, have a guilty conscience about their crime. Oh, they might try to rationalize it to themselves or try to justify their actions, but they know what they've done is wrong."

"Confession is the first step to redemption," Abby mused.

"I believe there's good in all people," Henry said. "Only sometimes it's buried deep down inside of them, under layers of greed or selfishness or envy."

Abby knew most crimes were committed for those very reasons. It saddened her that more people didn't realize that true happiness couldn't be found by acquiring more money or material possessions.

"So when I'm interviewing a suspect," Henry continued, "I've found that silence is actually a very effective tool."

"You don't say anything?"

"Oh, maybe just enough to start them talking." He tipped up his cap. "You'd be amazed, Abby, at how sitting in a room with a guy who has a guilty conscience and not saying anything will drive him crazy. He's not sure what you know, so he tries to guess."

"I suppose that could be effective."

Henry nodded. "If the interview starts to drag, then I'll say just enough to make him start talking again. I ask open-ended questions, and more often than not, he's so busy trying to prove himself innocent that he does just the opposite by giving away too much information."

Abby was impressed by Henry's methods. "No wonder you're so good at your job."

He blushed at her compliment. "I do my best."

After Henry paid for the jewelry box and left the shop, Abby waited until Ana was in between customers before she approached her.

"This is a nice surprise," Ana said when she saw her. "How are you, Abby?"

"I'm fine," she replied. "How about you? Have you and Mateo recovered from your experience on *The Sea Prince*?"

Ana smiled. "We're both doing very well. Mateo has been busy telling everyone he knows about his exciting rescue at sea. It was a little too much excitement for me," she confessed. "I'm very happy to be back in my little shop where nothing too thrilling ever happens."

Abby thought that some of Ana's creations could be described as thrilling, but she didn't want to distract herself from the reason she'd come here. "Have you learned anything more about what happened on *The Sea Prince* that day?"

Ana shook her head. "Henry was just here asking me the same thing. Wondering if there was anything I'd seen or heard. But frankly, I was so busy trying to keep an eye on my little rascal of a grandson that I didn't even realize what was happening until the people around me started shouting."

Abby had assumed as much, but she couldn't help feeling disappointed.

"Although," Ana mused, her brow furrowed in deep thought, "now that I think about it, there was something strange that happened that day."

Another customer entered the shop, and Abby was left in suspense while Ana went to wait on him. A few minutes later, she returned to find Abby standing in the wood crafts aisle.

"Now where were we?" Ana pulled a dust rag out of her smock pocket. She began brushing it over an ornately carved wooden bench.

"You were telling me you saw something strange during your tour on *The Sea Prince*," Abby reminded her.

"That's right," Ana said, now moving her dust rag over a small rocking horse. "But this happened before the tour, not during it."

"Before you got on the boat?" Abby asked, making sure she understood her.

"Yes," Ana replied. "It was probably nothing, but it did startle me."

"What happened?"

"The strangest thing." Ana turned to face her. "I was doing a little scavenger hunting for craft material while Mateo and I were waiting in line to buy tickets. They were slow that day, because one of the ticket vendors had called in sick. Anyway, I saw a piece of driftwood floating in the water by the pilings. I'm always looking for pieces I can use for my crafts."

Abby had often seen Ana searching for driftwood and stones and such around the islands. Sometimes Ida Tolliver would accompany her, enjoying the unique treasure hunt.

"Anyway," Ana continued, "I about had a heart attack when I took the driftwood out of the water, because a scuba diver popped up right next to it."

"That would be frightening."

She nodded. "I certainly wasn't expecting to see him. He apologized for scaring me, though." Ana tapped her chin. "I wonder what he was doing in the water so early in the morning. It had to be cold."

"And this was near where *The Sea Prince* was docked?" Abby asked her.

"Only a few yards away."

"Did you recognize the scuba diver?"

Ana shook her head. "He was covered from head to toe in his wet suit and face mask. He could have been anyone."

Then her light brown eyes clouded with concern. "You don't think that scuba diver did something to *The Sea Prince* to make it sink do you?"

Abby didn't want to believe it, but she knew it should be investigated. "I don't know, Ana. I think you should tell Henry about it."

Ana nodded in agreement. "I will."

Abby looked around the shop. "I can never seem to walk in here without wanting to buy something." She ran her hand over the wooden quilt rack in front of her. "This is gorgeous."

"I've sold two already and have an order in for more." Ana headed toward the front counter. "Come and look at this."

Abby followed her and watched as Ana pulled out a box from behind the counter. "I just got a new shipment in today. They're the most beautiful brooches."

As she opened the box, Abby saw brooches carved out of tupelo wood that were similar to her own. There were birds, fish and whales of all shapes and colors.

"Aren't they nice?" Ana said, holding up an indigo bird against her smock. "They're made by Marshall Cox. He lives on Lopez Island and has a wood shop there. We sell each other's crafts on consignment. Best of all, he supplies me with lots of feathers free of charge."

"Really?" Abby said with a smile. "Does he like to go on scavenger hunts, too?"

"Oh no," Ana replied, "he gets the feathers from pigeons he keeps in his loft. He took me up there once. I've never seen so many birds all together in one place."

Abby's heart skipped a beat. "Pigeons?"

Ana nodded, then placed the brooch back in the box. "Homing pigeons. He releases them, and they take off for parts unknown, but they eventually come back to him. It's really quite interesting to hear him talk about it."

Tempted to run out of the store, Abby took a deep breath, telling herself this might not mean anything. Still, it was the best lead she'd had since Homer had crash-landed just outside her backyard.

"What's the name of his shop?" Abby asked her.

"The Woodchuck's Den," Ana tucked the dust cloth back into her smock. "Isn't that cute? If you decide to stop in there, tell Marshall I said hello."

"I'll do that," Abby promised as she headed toward the door. She also hoped to tell him that she had his homing pigeon.

CHAPTER ❧ SIXTEEN

Abby took the ferry to Lopez Island, then strolled the short distance to The Woodchuck's Den. When she walked inside, she inhaled the mingled scents of pine, cedar and sandalwood. One look around and Abby knew she'd walked into the shop of a true craftsman.

Finding herself alone in the store, Abby could hear the deep rumble of a man's voice from the back room. It gave her the opportunity to look around and gather some impressions of Marshall Cox.

His shop was tidy, the wood floor cleanly swept. He had a whimsical side, though, judging from the birds, airplanes and stars hanging from the rafters. She walked over to the front counter to look at the racing pigeon trophies on the shelf behind it. There were framed photographs of pigeons, too, and she wondered if one of them was Homer.

As she browsed through the store, she came across a carved wooden cross that had been lovingly etched with intricate detail. There were several nativity sets, too, and some beautiful wooden Bible cases.

Abby found it interesting how one could take stock of another person's life according to the items they chose to surround themselves with. She already found herself liking Marshall from the environment he'd created in The Woodchuck's Den. Hopefully, she'd feel the same way when she met the man in person.

Walking to the far corner of the shop, she found a large wooden porch swing set up. It stood on its own, with long wooden posts forming a triangle to support each end. A sign invited customers to try it out.

Abby took a seat, unable to resist the temptation.

Giving a small push on the floor with her foot, she began to swing back and forth, the gentle creak reminding her of days long past.

The motion comforted her as she leaned back against the smooth wooden seat. Closing her eyes, she wondered how long it had been since she'd just sat and enjoyed a lazy afternoon on a porch swing.

The sound of footsteps made her open her eyes to see a tall, burly man emerging from the back room. He looked to be in his late forties, and was wearing a red cotton shirt and faded denim jeans. His short, dark hair was streaked with silver, as was the beard on his face.

He didn't see Abby, seemingly lost in his thoughts as he walked over to his workbench and began to sand a long plank of oak.

She got up from the swing and cleared her throat, not wanting to startle him.

He turned around, then smiled when he saw her. "Oh, hello there. I didn't realize I had a customer."

"I was just enjoying your porch swing," Abby said, moving toward him. "It's so comfortable."

"They're custom-made," the man replied. "Whatever size and dimensions you like. I made one to fit a family of six just the other day."

Abby smiled, impressed with his marketing skills. That, combined with his talent as a craftsman probably made him a successful businessman. "I'm not in the market at the moment, but I'll definitely keep it in mind."

He put down the sanding block and picked up a towel to wipe the fine dust from his hands. "Is there anything I can help you find today?"

"Actually," Abby began, hoping her search was over, "I'm looking for Marshall Cox."

He tilted his head to one side, his green eyes curious. "You found him."

"My name is Abigail Stanton," she began, hoping he really was the man she was looking for. "I understand you like birds."

"I sure do." He pointed to the walnut bookcase next to him. A small bird was carved into each corner. "I guess I feel that birds and I are kindred spirits, since we both find comfort in trees. I even wait until a tree comes down naturally before I use it, since I just can't justify depriving a bird of its habitat."

Abby's opinion of the man soared. "Then we have something in common. I'm an ornithologist. I work as the Associate Curator at the Sparrow Island Nature Conservatory."

He nodded his approval. "Is that a fact? I've been there a time or two myself. I sure enjoyed your Wonderful World of Wings exhibit."

"Thank you," she said, quite proud of that accomplishment

herself. "The reason I'm here today is to talk to you about a very special bird. We call him Homer."

Marshall chuckled. "Nice to know I'm not the only one who likes to name birds. Though I have so many, sometimes it's hard to keep track of them all."

"Homer isn't my bird," Abby clarified. "He was found injured in the woods just outside my backyard. He's been recuperating at my laboratory in the conservatory ever since."

"What kind of bird is he?" Marshall asked.

Abby took in a deep breath. "A homing pigeon."

Marshall's face paled. "What?"

She took a step closer to him. "I came here on a hunch, Mr. Cox, because Ana Dominquez told me you raise homing pigeons. I've been looking for Homer's owner ever since we found him two weeks ago."

Marshall swallowed, still visibly shaken by her news. "Is he all right?"

"He's fine," Abby assured him. "Quite well, actually, though not ready to fly yet. We attempted to release him yesterday, but he just circled a few times, then came back to the conservatory."

Marshall walked over to the counter where he sagged onto a stool. "I think it must be Harold."

"Harold?" she echoed.

He nodded. "I thought something must have happened to him when he didn't come home on time. Frankly, I feared the worst. I can't believe that he's all right."

"Harold's fine," she assured him, knowing she'd need some time to get used to Homer's new name.

Marshall looked up at Abby, a smile curving beneath his beard.

"Harold always did like to take his time before another flight. It used to drive me crazy sometimes, but that's just his way."

Abby didn't say anything, sensing that Marshall needed someone to listen to him.

"I haven't seen Harold for so long," he continued. "I used to watch for him every day, and then . . ." He shook his head. "How was he injured? Do you have any idea what happened to him?"

"My best guess is that he was caught in a storm during the night and got off course. We found him the next day. He was quite weak. In fact, I wasn't sure he'd make it."

Marshall rubbed a hand over his face. "He's the last one that . . ." His voice trailed off again and Abby could see that he was upset.

She walked over to him, laying a comforting hand on his shoulder. "Are you all right, Mr. Cox?"

He sucked in a deep breath, then composed himself and nodded. "I'm fine. And please call me Marshall."

"All right, Marshall." Abby hesitated to tell him the rest, fearing it might upset him even more. But she knew she couldn't keep it from him forever.

Marshall looked up at her. "I need to go feed my pigeons. Would you like to come with me?"

Abby nodded, relieved to buy herself some time before breaking the news about the coded message. She was also curious to see Homer's—no, *Harold's* loft.

Marshall rose from the stool. "Then let's go."

ABBY RODE IN MARSHALL'S black Jeep Cherokee along winding gravel back roads on Lopez Island. They climbed higher and higher, leaving the more populated area of the island behind them.

At last they reached the top of a small ridge. On one side lay a small log cabin, on the other a steep cliff that led to the water below.

"This is my home," Marshall said, climbing out of the driver's seat. "Small but cozy."

"It's lovely." Abby joined him on the dirt path that led to the back of the house. "The view here is amazing."

He nodded his agreement. "I love looking out at the sound. The steady rhythm of the waves is so comforting. Sometimes it feels as if God is rocking me to sleep at night."

Abby smiled to herself at that image. Marshall was a big, burly man, but still turned to his faith for comfort. That made him seem even stronger in her eyes.

Marshall led her around the back of the log cabin, where he kept his pigeon loft. It looked big enough to house a small family and the way he interacted with his pigeons made Abby believe he thought of them as his children.

The birds began to coo and flap against the mesh enclosure as soon as they saw Marshall appear.

The pigeon loft was mounted about a foot and a half off the ground. Half the building was open, covered only by a wire mesh fabric. It reminded Abby of a screen porch that allowed in the sun and breeze while the sturdy roof protected the pigeons from rain.

Abby smiled at the chorus as the birds flocked to the feeding room that was set up at one end of the building.

"Dinnertime," Marshall called out, scooping a mixture of grain and pellets out of a barrel. He poured it into the feed troughs and Abby noted with approval that he had enough of them to prevent overcrowding.

She could tell by the cleanliness of the water containers and the grit containers in the feeding room that Marshall took good care of his birds.

"This is quite an impressive setup," she said, watching him work.

Marshall nodded his thanks. "I built it about three years ago. This west section is the feed room and the east section is divided into individual rooms to house the hens, cocks and young birds. The wire mesh keeps out any predators."

"What is that?" Abby asked, pointing to a four-foot by eight-foot board that ran vertically along one side of the building.

"That's a landing board," Marshall explained. "It's a way for the pigeons to get back into the loft after a long journey."

Now Abby could see the small holes behind the landing board that allowed just enough room for the pigeons to enter the loft. "They certainly seem happy to see you."

He smiled. "I probably spoil them too much, but I can't seem to help myself." He began to point out individual birds to her. "This is Desdemona and that's Gerald. Over there are Winona and Donald. Lisette and Louis."

"Any chicks from the happy couples yet?" Abby asked.

He laughed at her question. "Quite a few, actually. Pigeons mate for life, you know." Then he rolled his eyes. "Of course, you do. You're an ornithologist."

Marshall's mood had improved considerably. Abby could see that his pigeons brought him joy. "So does Homer have a mate?"

His smile widened. "You mean Harold?"

She shook her head at her own forgetfulness. "Well, we got the first letter of his name right anyway."

"Yes, he does," Marshall replied. "Her name is Irene and she's right over there."

Abby observed Harold's mate while Marshall turned his attention back to his birds, responding to their coos with gentle words.

At last, Abby knew she couldn't delay any longer. Reaching for her bag, she pulled out the coded message that Homer had been carrying when Finnegan found him.

"Homer . . . I mean Harold," she corrected herself, wondering if she'd ever get it right, "was carrying this message when we found him." Abby held the note out to Marshall. "It was in code."

He hesitated a moment, then took the note from her, but he didn't look at it. "Do you know what it says?"

A blush warmed her cheeks. "We did decipher it, hoping it might help us discover Homer's owner."

Marshall gave a brisk nod. "She dumped me, didn't she?"

Abby blinked, confused for a moment. "What?"

"The message," he clarified. "Didn't she say it was over?"

"No," Abby replied, finally understanding. "Whoever wrote that note wanted to meet with you. We didn't understand exactly where or when, but . . ."

Marshall didn't wait to hear the rest of what she had to say. Pulling open the message, his gaze scanned the code.

"*Time is running out,*" he read aloud. "*Meet at loft on day we parted.*"

Abby was impressed by his quick translation skills. Then she saw the look of anguish on his face and her heart ached for him.

"I'm so sorry I didn't find you sooner," she said softly.

He closed his eyes for a moment, his head bowed. Then he took a deep breath and looked up to meet her gaze. "Two days ago. She was *right here* two days ago. And that's the day I decided to go to Seattle to buy bird supplies."

Abby didn't say anything, unwilling to push Marshall to share more of his story than he wished.

"It's not your fault," he said at last. "You did more than anyone could expect."

"Are you sure it's too late?" Abby asked him. "Maybe she's still on the island."

He shook his head. "We probably should have given up years ago."

Abby watched him pick Irene out of the flock of pigeons and cradle her against his chest.

"Tessa March and I met in high school," Marshall said, a faraway look in his eyes. "We had to do a science fair project together and she suggested we buy a homing pigeon and train it. Her father had trained the birds in World War II, so he gave us a lot of advice."

Abby listened to his story unfold, imagining the two young teenagers. If Marshall was in his forties now, that meant their relationship had spanned almost thirty years.

"Our fathers were in business together," he continued, "but something happened and they had a falling out. They hated each other after that. Tessa and I would meet secretly. We were in love. We even made plans to elope after graduation."

"But that didn't happen?"

He sighed. "Her father became ill with multiple sclerosis. He had to sell his house and move back to Ohio. Tessa knew he didn't have anyone to take care of him so she went with him."

"And you never saw her again?"

He shook his head. "We wrote to each other at first, but when her father saw one of my letters, he became very upset. He thought she was going to leave him. He had to be hospitalized."

"Oh no," Abby cried, imagining the guilt the young girl must have felt.

"That's when I got the first message by homing pigeon. She'd taken Dover, that was the bird from our science project, along with her to Ohio. She attached a note to Dover's leg. A few weeks later the pigeon arrived here, at her old home. I'd started raising homing pigeons myself by then."

"So you continued communicating with each other via homing pigeon?"

He nodded. "We even developed this secret code in case her father ever came across one of our messages again. She didn't want him to have another attack."

"But a homing pigeon's life span is only three to five years in the wild and maybe ten to fifteen in captivity," Abby said. "How did you continue to communicate over thirty years?"

"I sent a young pigeon along with Dover when she set off for Ohio again. When that pigeon was trained, another went with it. And so on."

Abby was amazed at their long correspondence by homing pigeon. They must truly be devoted to each other. "Why did you say it was over? Can't you just call Tessa and explain? Set up a meeting with her?"

He shook his head. "I don't know where to find her. I tried to call the house in Ohio about a month ago, when I read the notice of her father's death in the newspaper. The phone number had been disconnected."

Abby could hear the defeat in his voice.

"I still love her," he declared, "but I thought I was respecting her wishes by letting her move on with her life."

After thirty years, he'd come to believe that they were never meant to be together. Abby's heart went out to the young couple who had been torn apart by circumstances beyond their control.

"I thought she'd given up on me." He looked at the wrinkled message in his hand. "Until I saw this."

Abby was amazed at his story. And deeply saddened that it had to end this way. She walked with him to the front yard and stood in silence at the cliff top, watching the waves below.

"Thank you again for everything," he said softly, his gaze on the water. "Do you mind if I come by the conservatory on Monday and get Harold?"

"Not at all," she replied. "I know he'll be happy to see you again."

She turned to leave when something caught her eye. It was a boat anchored offshore.

"Funny, isn't it," Marshall said, catching her gaze. "That's about the worst place around here to weigh anchor. That boat catches the worst of the north wind and spends half the day in the shadow of the cliff."

"Must be someone who likes his privacy," Abby guessed.

"Hardly," Marshall scoffed. "It's that hotshot who's on the news all the time lately. The guy who's looking for the missing orca calf. Looks to me like he enjoys the spotlight."

"Mick Wymore?" Abby said, squinting into the distance. "Are you sure?"

"Positive," Marshall replied. "One of his crewmen came into my shop a while back and was complaining that this trip to the San Juan Islands wasn't at all what he'd expected. Said they just sit in the same place all the time. That sailor hasn't been back though, so maybe he found a more exciting job."

Abby wondered if the odd location had anything to do with Mick's doctoral research. Though now that she thought about it, he hadn't mentioned his research in quite a while. His focus seemed to be entirely on the missing orca calf and the publicity surrounding it.

"I'd like to give you something before you leave," Marshall said. "As a sort of thank-you gift for taking care of Harold."

"That isn't necessary," she assured him, touched by the gesture.

But Marshall refused to take no for an answer. "I insist, Abby. Please just wait right here. I'll be back in a flash."

Abby watched the waves for a few more minutes, her gaze returning to Mick's boat. She knew he lived on board and came ashore on a dingy, but Abby realized she'd never asked him where he was anchored.

Marshall emerged from the house carrying a beautifully carved walking stick. Her eyes widened when she saw it.

"Here," he said, presenting it to her.

"Oh, I couldn't take this," Abby protested, even as her hands caressed the silky smooth wood. The walking stick was a little over three feet long and was intricately decorated with a flock of seabirds spiraling upward to the top. She knew he must have worked for days to create something this lovely.

"Please do," he insisted. "You've found Harold for me and given me—" his voice cracked, "closure. Now that it's over, I can move on."

The expression on his face belied his words. Pigeons mated for life and something told Abby that Tessa was the only woman that Marshall would ever want or love. She took the walking stick, not wanting to hurt his feelings by rejecting his gift.

"Thank you, Marshall" she said sincerely, "I'll always treasure it."

Then she turned her head away, fearing that she might start crying herself. She would have to pull herself together and ask for a ride back to town. She'd accomplished her mission of finding Homer—no, *Harold*—his home, only to discover that Tessa March was now lost.

CHAPTER ❧ SEVENTEEN

ABBY COULDN'T GET HER mind off of Tessa and Marshall's plight the rest of the weekend. She and Bobby said their good-byes to Homer/Harold when Marshall came to pick him up on Monday, then she busied herself with adding some framed photographs of birds and wildlife to the workroom walls of The Nature Museum.

Taking down a couple of the older pictures, she placed them in the workroom closet, along with the walking stick Marshall had given her, not sure where else to store it. The walking stick was so beautifully made that Abby wasn't sure she'd ever use it. She'd hate for it to get scratched or dirty while out on one of the trails.

As she left the museum that evening, Abby almost bumped into a man standing right outside the door.

"Excuse me," she said, looking up into his face. Then she almost dropped her bag when she saw Judd Peavey standing in front of her.

"We need to talk," the sailor said gruffly. "In private."

She turned back toward the building. "We can go into my office."

He shook his head. "I'd rather stay outside. I get claustrophobic if I'm cooped in somewhere."

Since Judd looked as if he could bolt at any moment, Abby was eager to accommodate him. "Then let's take a walk by the creek," she suggested. "No one should bother us there."

He consented with a brisk nod of his head, then let her lead the way. Abby took him on the path that led to the creek, the fine gravel crunching under their shoes. Judd didn't speak as they walked, though he did study the plants and flowers that were marked with small signs along the way.

She walked silently beside him, sensing that Judd was not a man to be pushed into talking before he was ready. But the longer they walked, the more she worried that he was having second thoughts about meeting with her. What if he changed his mind and ran off?

"That Barney is a pain in the neck," Judd grumbled at last.

They stood by the creek, watching the water tumble over the rocks. "He said he wouldn't leave me alone until I came and talked to you."

"I appreciate it," Abby said, trying to put him at ease. "You can trust me, Judd."

He kicked a pebble with the toe of his boot. "There's one thing you gotta promise before I say anything. I want my name kept out of it. Understood?"

"Understood," Abby affirmed. She knew the close brotherhood among sailors and realized that Judd felt that talking to her was a type of betrayal. She hoped that someday he would understand that whoever had sailed through the orca pod had used that sense of loyalty to his advantage.

"Here's the thing," Judd began. "I didn't just see the boat that cut through the K pod that night, I was on it."

Abby stepped back in surprise. "So it was *The Sea Prince*?" she said, aware that Judd was a former crewman. "That means Captain Zirka's responsible for disturbing the K pod and injuring Rosie."

Judd shook his head. "No, Zirka had nothing to do with it. He was too drunk most of the time to know what was going on. In fact, he was passed out cold the night it happened. He wasn't even on the boat."

"Then who did it?" Abby asked, looking up at the sailor.

Judd hesitated, a muscle twitching in his jaw. She could see the fierce battle inside of him reflected on his weathered face.

"Please, Judd," she said, laying a gentle hand on his forearm. "I know this isn't easy for you, but I need to know what happened that night. The mother orca was injured and almost died. Poppy's still missing."

"I know that," Judd spat out. "Don't you think that's been haunting me ever since it happened? We weren't told he planned to sail right through the K pod. Only that he wanted to stir things up a bit around here."

Abby wasn't sure what that meant, but she didn't push Judd to explain. Instead, she stood silently beside him, hoping he would tell her more of his own accord.

"He picked his midnight crew well. We were all men who had something in our past that we wanted to hide. He offered to pay us good money, but also made it clear that he'd spread our secrets far and wide if we didn't cooperate. We had jobs at stake . . . families . . ." His voice trailed off, then he shook his head. "I know that doesn't begin to justify what we did."

Abby could imagine the turmoil of the men. Now she realized that the reason for his reticence wasn't loyalty, but shame.

"Did you know what he intended to do that night?"

He met her gaze, his eyes imploring her to believe him. "None of us knew he planned to sail straight through the K pod. Then it happened." He shuddered. "I'll never forget that awful sound when he hit the orca."

Abby wanted to comfort him, but she chose to listen and let him release the guilt and anguish inside of him.

"He took *The Luna* out that night, too," Judd continued in a low voice. "Just long enough to crash it into a rock. He had it all planned out."

Abby could only stare at him, chilled by the recount of such a calculating scheme.

"So that's it," he told her, raking a hand through his shaggy brown hair. "It was a setup to get rid of the Andersons, as well as Zirka and his tour boat. Only it backfired when Breslin bought *The Sea Prince* and added it to his line."

"So this was all about money?" Abby asked, confirming what she'd suspected all along. "About getting rid of the competition?"

Judd nodded. "At the price of the mother orca and her calf." Anger blazed in his gray eyes. "I'll never forgive myself for becoming involved with that man. I've already donated the money he paid me to The Whale Museum, but that doesn't make up for what I did."

"You're wrong," she told him gently. "You're already making up for it by talking to me. And by donating the money he gave you. I happen to think you're a good man, Judd."

He sighed, a wistful look in his eyes. "Maybe not yet, but I'm going to be."

She believed him. Abby just wished he'd come to her sooner.

Then maybe the near-tragedy with *The Sea Prince* could have been avoided.

"That's all I came to say," Judd announced, his stiff shoulders relaxing as if a huge weight had been lifted from them.

But there was still one thing that Abby needed to know. "Who was it, Judd? Who paid you to sail through the K pod?"

He met her gaze. "Captain Lewis Hovel."

TWENTY MINUTES LATER, Abby entered the sheriff's substation looking for Henry. She knew he was working with the Coast Guard to investigate the orca pod disturbance and wanted to let him know what she'd learned from Judd.

She found Henry at his desk, a pile of folders in front of him. "I hope I'm not interrupting anything too important."

"Actually, I could use a break." He put down his pen and smiled up at her. "I'm just catching up on some paperwork. Amazing how it can pile up on you when you're not looking."

"I feel the same way about my paperwork at the conservatory. I'd much rather be leading a birding tour than filling out forms."

"What brings you here, Abby?" Henry asked her.

She took a seat across the desk from him. "I just talked to someone who was on the boat that sailed through the K pod."

His expression sobered as he leaned forward. "Who was it?"

"He asked me to keep his name confidential," she explained. "But it was a sailor who was specifically hired, along with some others, to disturb the orca pod."

Henry sank back in his chair. "I kept wanting to believe it was an accident, but it just never added up. Did this confidential source happen to tell you who was behind it?"

"Captain Lewis Hovel," Abby replied. "Apparently, he hired

a group of sailors with shady pasts and convinced them to run *The Sea Prince* through the K pod. He wanted to get rid of some of his competition in the whale-watching tour business."

"*The Sea Prince*?" Henry exclaimed.

Abby nodded. "He also caused the damage to *The Luna*." Then another thought occurred to her. "Do you suppose the collision with Rosie caused enough damage to *The Sea Prince* to cause it to start sinking the other day?"

"It's possible," Henry surmised. "Though it seems odd *The Sea Prince* didn't start taking on water right after the incident."

"Whatever happened," Abby said, "I'm sure Captain Breslin didn't know about the damage when he bought the boat or he never would have taken *The Sea Prince* out on the water. At least, I hope he wouldn't."

"I think you're right about that. I interviewed Kyle Breslin after it happened, and he told me that was the first outing of *The Sea Prince* since his purchase."

"It still doesn't make sense to me," Abby mused. "That Captain Hovel would put all those people in danger just to win a few extra passengers."

"The problem is we still don't have any definitive proof that he's behind it," Henry said. "Especially if this source of yours wants to remain confidential."

Abby sighed. "I don't think he'll testify, if that's what you're asking. It was hard enough for him to tell *me* what happened."

"Then what about Dennis Zirka?" Henry picked up the accident report in front of him. "As the former captain of *The Sea Prince*, he might have some useful information for us."

"Captain Zirka has a drinking problem and was incapacitated that night. Although, my guess is that he heard about the incident, then discovered the damage to his boat and put two and two together. Maybe that's why he sold *The Sea Prince* so quickly and disappeared."

Henry steepled his hands together, mulling over her story. "I have to admit that we'd already excluded Captain Hovel as a suspect in this case. I did that background check you asked for on Captain Zirka and he has plenty of citations in his past. He was my top suspect."

"Does that mean you cleared the Andersons?"

Henry sorted through the files on his desk, then handed one to her. "The report just came in today. The damage to *The Luna* was sustained by a rock, not the orca, which is just more proof that it was done intentionally."

Abby looked over the file, relieved that the Andersons had been cleared. She knew their reputation had suffered and that that would take longer to repair. "But can we prove Captain Hovel is responsible for this, too?"

Henry shrugged. "We'll certainly try. If he wanted to get rid of his competition, this was one way to do it. Not only did he involve Zirka's boat in this mess, but he implicated *The Luna* as well."

"But if none of the sailors involved are willing to talk," Abby said in frustration, "then there's nothing to tie Captain Hovel to the incident with the K pod or *The Luna* since his boat wasn't even involved."

"We'll know soon enough what caused *The Sea Prince* to founder. Kyle Breslin was in earlier today and insisted that the boat be dry-docked, along with *The Polaris*, to rule out any evidence of foul play."

"Kyle seems like a good young man," Abby replied. "I'm glad to know he's willing to let investigators take a look at his boats."

Henry nodded. "I agree. It's a shame he and the Andersons have been dragged into this case when they're innocent of any wrongdoing."

The more she thought about it, the more Abby realized how much damage Captain Hovel had done, not only to Rosie, Poppy and the orca pod, but to people like Kyle, the Andersons, Judd and even Captain Zirka. All for his own selfish gain.

Henry picked up his pen and started jotting down some notes. "I'll do a background check on Hovel. Maybe we can find something there. And I'll let the Coast Guard know what's going on. That way at least they can keep an eye on him from now on."

Abby didn't even want to consider the possibility that Captain Hovel might get away with it. There had to be something more she could do to bring him to justice.

"Anything new to report on the missing orca calf?" Henry asked her.

She swallowed a sigh. "Nothing yet, I'm afraid. What puzzles me the most is that with all this publicity, there haven't been any sightings of Poppy. She can't be that far from home."

Henry rose to his feet. "I guess we have to accept the fact that we may never find her."

But Abby wasn't ready to surrender yet. She wasn't going to give up hope of finding the orca calf or bringing Captain Hovel to justice. She wasn't going to let Marshall give up, either. Not when she might be able to do something about it.

Abby was still motivated when she got home that evening. She found Mary in her craft room, working on an elaborate dried flower arrangement.

"Are you ready to do some brainstorming?" Abby asked her.

Mary's eyes widened as Abby marched into the room with

a notebook, an atlas and a telephone book in her arms. "What's gotten into you?"

"We're going to find Marshall's long lost love, Tessa March."

Mary put down the glue bottle. "Okay, back up there a minute, sis. Who is Marshall?"

As soon as Abby had returned from her visit with Marshall on Saturday, she had told Mary every detail of their meeting and how Marshall had missed meeting Tessa because they didn't find him in time to give him the note.

"I've been thinking a lot about their plight," Mary said. "A thirty-year, long-distance romance. They must be so devoted to one another."

Abby flipped open the notebook on her lap. "Unfortunately, time has taken its toll. They've started to doubt each other now, and if we don't do something they may never get together."

Mary smiled at her determination. "So you want us to play matchmaker?"

Abby laughed, realizing how she must have looked when she'd marched into the room. "Okay, I know these two people are basically strangers to us, but Marshall's a very nice man. And I feel responsible somehow. If we had decoded the note sooner, maybe we would have found him in time for him to make the meeting with Tessa."

Mary rolled her wheelchair over to where Abby sat. "Hey, I'm willing to give it a try. Where do we look first?"

"That's a good question." Abby opened her notebook. "I think we should start with Ohio. Surely someone there knows where she moved. A neighbor or her bank or even the post office."

Mary took the atlas from her and opened it to Ohio. "What town was she in?"

"I don't know," Abby replied, suddenly realizing she was short on facts about Tessa. All she knew was her name and the state she'd moved to thirty years ago.

"Well, we have to start somewhere," Mary said. "Do you have any guesses?"

The futility of their mission suddenly struck Abby and she got up to stand by the window. Even if they did an Internet search there was no guarantee they would find the right Tessa March. "Here's what I don't understand."

"What?" Mary asked.

Abby turned around to face her. "Why would Tessa come all the way to the San Juan Islands, then leave without seeing Marshall?"

Mary looked as perplexed as Abby felt. "A case of nerves, maybe. Or perhaps she feared Marshall didn't love her anymore, especially when he didn't show up for their meeting at the loft."

"But she was there," Abby mused, something niggling at her. "Someone might have seen her or talked to her. Maybe she even stayed around for a few days. . . ." Her voice trailed off as one of the pieces of this puzzle suddenly fell into place for her.

"What is it?" Mary said, seeing her expression. "Is something wrong?"

"No, just the opposite, in fact." Abby's heart began to pound. Could it really be this simple? "I was at The Dorset to see Peggy Endorf, remember?"

"Yes, I remember," Mary replied. "And?"

"And it was filled with people going to the vigil. One of the people I talked to on the elevator was a girl wearing a *SAVE POPPY!* T-shirt."

"You told me about her," Mary said. "She sounded like one of Mick's groupies."

Abby nodded. "But I talked to another woman on the elevator, too. She wasn't going to the vigil. She told me she was going to a reunion."

Mary's eyes widened. "A reunion with Marshall Cox?"

"I think it's possible. The woman's name was Teresa. Maybe when she was younger, people called her Tessa."

"Do you really think the woman you met on the elevator could be Tessa March?"

"I'm almost sure it was her," Abby replied. "She wore a small wooden pendant with an engraving of a bird on it. Wood crafts are Marshall's business."

Abby knew Mary would see his talent for herself when Henry presented her with the jewelry box. But she wasn't about to spoil the surprise.

"So what do we do now?" Mary asked, catching Abby's excitement. "Tell Marshall?"

Abby thought about it for a moment, then shook her head. "I don't want to get his hopes up in case we're wrong. In fact, Teresa might have left the island already. She didn't mention how long she was staying."

"Well, let's find out," Mary said, reaching for the telephone. "Call The Dorset and ask if she's still there."

Abby looked up the number, then dialed the hotel. It rang six times before someone finally picked up.

"The Dorset," said a young man's voice on the other end of the line. "How may I help you?"

"I'm looking for someone," Abby said, so nervous that her mouth was dry. She licked her lips, then continued. "Her name is Teresa March, and I believe she's a guest at your hotel."

"One moment, please." Then he put her on hold.

The next few minutes dragged on forever. Mary sat beside her, hugging the atlas in her arms.

"Hello?" the young man said.

Abby cleared her throat. "Yes, I'm still here."

"We do have a guest registered by that name staying at the hotel. She's due to check out tomorrow at noon. Would you like me to connect you?"

Abby wanted to jump for joy. Teresa March had to be Tessa March. "No, thank you very much."

When she hung up, Mary said, "Well?"

"Teresa's last name is March and she's still on the island." Abby began to pace the room, filled with nervous energy. "I thought about talking to her on the telephone, but I think I should do it in person. Don't you?"

"Definitely," Mary affirmed. "You don't know how she'll react. Or even if she's the Tessa March you're looking for."

Abby glanced at her watch. "I'll head over there right after supper. I'm afraid if I wait until tomorrow I might miss her."

"Good idea," Mary agreed. "I wonder why she's staying on Sparrow Island instead of Lopez Island. Isn't that where Marshall lives?"

"Yes," Abby replied. "And I don't know the answer. Maybe I'll find out tonight."

Mary headed toward the kitchen. "Then I'd better set dinner on the table so you can be on your way."

Abby wasn't sure she could eat anything. The revelation about Captain Hovel as well as her theory that the woman staying at The Dorset might be Tessa March had her stomach in knots.

If it was Tessa, then Marshall could finally have his happy

ending. Abby just wished she could say the same for the missing orca calf.

With each passing day, it seemed less likely that Poppy would survive the long separation from her mother and the rest of the K pod.

Maybe it was time for Abby to accept the fact that Poppy might be lost forever.

CHAPTER ❧ EIGHTEEN

Abby walked into the Dorset later that evening, surprised to find the lobby much less crowded than the last time she'd been here. Then again, Mick didn't have any more candlelight vigils planned.

To her surprise, as she approached the front desk, she saw the blonde woman from the elevator standing right in front of her.

Abby's pulse quickened as she waited, wanting to let the woman finish her business with the clerk.

As Abby stood there, she wondered how to broach the subject of Marshall. If this woman wasn't the Tessa March she was looking for, Abby would sound like a complete loon.

She smiled to herself, realizing it wouldn't be the first time that had happened, or likely the last. Taking risks was often the way to reap the greatest rewards, even if one felt foolish in the process.

Teresa thanked the clerk at the desk, then turned around and saw Abby. Her eyes widened with recognition and she spoke first.

"Oh, hello again," Teresa said, walking toward her. "Abby, right?"

"That's right." Abby replied. "I was wondering if I could have a few minutes of your time."

Teresa looked surprised by the question. "Sure, I don't have any plans at the moment."

"Good." Abby motioned to a pair of wing chairs in the corner of the room. "Shall we sit down?"

Teresa followed her there, a puzzled expression on her face. "Do you mind if I ask what you want to talk to me about?"

Abby took a seat, then waited for Teresa to do the same before she spoke. "This may sound strange, but I've been looking for someone and I think you may be her."

Teresa frowned. "I still don't understand."

Realizing she was making a mess of it, Abby tried again. "I found an injured homing pigeon about two weeks ago. He was carrying a coded message."

Teresa's face paled. "You found Harold?"

"Yes," she replied, thrilled that her instincts had been correct. "He's alive and well. So you're Tessa March?"

The woman nodded, bewilderment in her green eyes. "So Harold was injured and you got the message? That means—" Her words cut off as she realized the implication and tears filled her eyes.

Abby reached out and squeezed Tessa's hand. "Marshall never got your message. He didn't know you were waiting to meet him."

Tessa covered her face with both hands, her shoulders shaking as she silently wept. "I waited at the loft for over an hour, but he never showed up. I thought it was over. I didn't know he never got the message."

The garbled words were drowned in her tears and Abby could do nothing but tenderly pat her knee to comfort her. They received a few curious glances from the staff and guests, but Tessa was completely unaware of it.

At last, Tessa reached into her purse and withdrew a tissue, wiping her tear-streaked face with it. "I'm sorry. I don't know what came over me. I just—" her voice cracked and for a moment Abby thought she was going to start crying again.

But Teresa sucked in one deep breath, then another, to retain control. "Please tell me everything. From the beginning."

So Abby began the story from the moment Finnegan had alerted them to the presence of Homer and continued through her meeting with Marshall on Saturday.

Tessa listened with rapt attention, tearing up when she heard about Harold's injuries and again when Abby told her about Marshall's reaction to finding her note too late and missing their reunion.

"These past few days," Tessa breathed, shaking her head in wonder, "I thought he just didn't want to see me. That he wanted to make a clean break of it. I stayed on here longer than I intended just to try and work up the courage to go and see him face-to-face."

"And?" Abby said.

Tessa gave her a wan smile. "And I chickened out. I'm headed back to Boston tomorrow morning. That's where I relocated after my father's death to help my cousin run her shoe store."

"Even though you came all this way to see Marshall?" Abby wondered at the couple's reticence with each other after keeping up a correspondence for three decades. "Were you really going to leave without seeing him?"

Tessa released a deep sigh. "It's hard to explain, Abby. We've been apart for so long—almost thirty years. When he didn't show up for our meeting, I thought maybe it was for the best. I mean, look at me."

She gazed down at her body with dismay. "I'm twenty pounds overweight, not the skinny young girl he remembers. I color my hair now to cover the gray and I need to wear bifocals when I read. The only reason I stayed here at The Dorset instead of on Lopez Island was so I wouldn't accidentally run into him." Her voice dropped to a whisper. "He probably wouldn't even recognize me now."

Abby finally understood Tessa's fear and probably Marshall's as well. They hadn't seen each other for so long that each was afraid the other would be disappointed. They'd rather believe their love had faded than face a possible rejection.

"Do you still love Marshall?" Abby asked her bluntly.

Tessa nodded. "With all my heart."

"He told me that he loves you too," Abby said gently. "Don't you think he deserves a chance to see the woman you've become?"

Tessa looked wistful. "For so many years, Marshall was my only real connection to the outside world. I used to be thrilled when one of the pigeons would arrive with a message from him—a message about our future together." She folded her hands on her lap. "But my father was very ill. He had multiple sclerosis and needed constant care."

Abby nodded, knowing how quickly an illness or accident could change someone's life. She thought of her sister and how that car accident had left her in a wheelchair, though Mary was still strong in mind and spirit.

"I loved my father so much," Tessa said, her eyes glistening with unshed tears. "He'll always hold a special place in my heart."

"It must be difficult," Abby said softly, "to find yourself alone now."

"I used to dream about having a chance to start my life over with Marshall again," Tessa confessed, "but it's been so long since we've seen each other or really talked to each other. Maybe I've let my dreams distort reality."

Abby could hear the uncertainty wavering in her voice. "Change is always scary, but we have to trust ourselves—and God—that we're on the right path."

Tessa considered her words for a long moment and met Abby's gaze. "I know we've just met, but I'm hoping you'll do me a favor."

"If I can."

"Will you take me to Marshall? Not tonight," she added quickly. "I need to get myself ready. How about tomorrow?"

"We can take the morning ferry over to Lopez Island," Abby suggested.

Tessa hesitated a moment, then nodded her head. "All right. I don't know what the future holds for us, but I think I'm finally ready to take the first step."

Abby smiled. "I'll be happy to lead the way."

ABBY DIDN'T SLEEP WELL that night and got up early the next morning to spend some extra time during her devotional. She found comfort in the Book of Proverbs:

"Trust in the Lord with all your heart and lean not on your own understanding; in all your ways acknowledge him, and he will make your paths straight" (Proverbs 3:5–6).

After a quick breakfast, Abby decided she had time to stop

by the conservatory and check on her birds before meeting Teresa at the ferry. Her plan was disrupted when she was met in the conservatory parking lot by none other than Captain Lewis Hovel.

"I've been waiting for you," he said as she climbed out of her car.

Abby turned around to see him standing behind her, her heart in her throat. A quick glance around the parking lot told her they were alone. "What do you want?"

He took a menacing step toward her. "I want to know why you seem so intent on destroying me."

After seeing him in action with his crew, she knew he was a bully. He was trying to bully her now and Abby realized the best way to counter his attack was not to let him intimidate her.

She squared her shoulders. "It seems to me that you are the one intent on destruction, Captain Hovel. You blackmailed a crew of men to sail *The Sea Prince* through the K pod and you've been trying to cover your tracks ever since."

His gaze narrowed on her. "It's no business of yours what I do, lady. You got that?"

"The orcas are my business," she retorted. "The tourists on *The Sea Prince* are my business. Any time someone is hurt or in danger it's up to others to step in and help. Especially when one of your victims is a defenseless orca calf."

He smiled, but she could see the anger in his eyes. "You don't have one shred of proof that *I* did anything. Your so-called witness has a history of lying and cheating. Now he's going around trying to talk other sailors into backing up his story."

Abby's heart ached for Judd. His confession to Abby must have given him courage to face the consequences of his actions and seek redemption. His wish for anonymity was now trumped by his desire to be believed.

"Well, it's not going to work," Captain Hovel snarled. "I have a stellar reputation that will stand up against any dirty lie."

"If you're innocent, then you have nothing to worry about," Abby told him. "So why are you here?"

He pointed a finger in her face. "I'm here to let you know that you'd better watch yourself, Dr. Stanton. When you get involved with people like Judd Peavey, bad things begin to happen."

His tone made her skin prickle. "Is that a threat, Captain Hovel?"

Before he could reply, another car pulled up next to Abby's and Mick emerged from the driver's seat.

"Hello, there," he called out.

Hovel glared at Abby. "You've been warned." Then he spun on his heel and walked away.

Mick approached her, his face quizzical. "What was that all about?"

She took a deep breath, a little shaken by the encounter. "I have reason to believe that Captain Hovel is responsible for sailing through the K pod and injuring the mother orca."

"No way," Mick countered. "Captain Hovel's not that stupid."

She was a little surprised by his quick defense of the man. "I think the reason has more to do with greed than stupidity."

"You're right about that," Mick agreed, "but it's not Captain Hovel who's responsible. Last night, I was talking to one of the sailors who used to work on *The Sea Prince*. It sounds like Captain Zirka had some serious problems."

Abby knew from her conversation with Judd that this was true, but she let Mick continue without interruption.

"Drinking and gambling himself deep into debt," Mick said with a note of disgust in his voice. "When Captain Zirka accidentally rammed that mother orca, he knew his hull might be seriously damaged and he didn't have any insurance on it."

"What sailor did you talk to?" Abby said, disturbed by the conflicting accounts.

Mick shrugged. "I never heard his real name. His friends called him Slick. The point is that Captain Zirka made a quick sale to Kyle Breslin and got out of Dodge."

Abby couldn't argue with that unsettling detail. Now she didn't know what to think. The sailor Mick had talked to could be lying, but so could Judd, despite his apparent sincerity.

"Think about it," Mick said, sensing her confusion. "What better way to clear Captain Zirka than to implicate someone else? This sailor worked for Zirka at one time, right?"

Abby nodded, wondering now if she'd been wrong to give Judd Peavey the benefit of the doubt. He'd been so adamant about keeping his name confidential, yet the next day everyone seemed to know about it. Was this just a gambit in a larger scheme? A plan to deflect suspicion away from the absent Captain Zirka?

"Zirka's probably paying him off," Mick continued. "I mean, what sense does it make for Captain Hovel to commandeer *The Sea Prince* and sail through the K pod? How would he ever keep that a secret?"

"It may not be a secret much longer," Abby replied. "*The Sea Prince* will be dry-docked soon. If there's any damage to her hull consistent with hitting the mother orca, we'll know about it."

"That may be." Mick considered the problem. "But we still won't know who was responsible. Captain Hovel's denying it and Captain Zirka's not here to defend himself. If I had to choose the man who did it, I'd accuse the one who ran away."

Abby knew most people would feel the same way. Yet, Mick hadn't seen the look on Captain Hovel's face when he'd talked to her just now. Nor had he heard the veiled threat. "If Captain Hovel's innocent, then why is he so upset with me?"

Mick shrugged. "I can't speak for the man. Although if I were unjustly accused of something as egregious as injuring a mother orca and causing her baby to go missing, I'd probably be upset too."

"I suppose you're right," Abby admitted, still not ready to absolve Captain Hovel. At least, not until she had definite proof that Captain Zirka was to blame. She just didn't know how to acquire that proof.

They started walking toward the museum. "What brings you here today?" she asked Mick.

"I'm meeting Hugo for breakfast," he replied. "You're welcome to join us."

Abby wondered if Hugo was going to pitch his job offer to Mick. "Thank you, but I have an important errand to run this morning."

They walked in silence for a few moments, then Mick turned to her and said, "Look, I know Captain Hovel's a little rough around the edges, but I think deep down he's a good guy. He was one of the first to welcome me here and offer to show me the location of the orca pods for my research."

Abby admired Mick's defense of the man, even if she didn't feel the same. Captain Hovel could be charming when he wished—she'd learned that the first night she'd met him. She'd also learned that the man had a quick temper, which had been on display again this morning.

"I think we should hold off accusing anyone," Mick continued, "until we hear the results of *The Sea Prince* investigation. There might be some new evidence that points to Zirka or to Hovel. Then we'll know for sure."

"You're right," Abby replied, not ready to publicly accuse Captain Hovel yet. She hadn't intended to talk to anyone except Henry about her suspicions, until Captain Hovel had confronted her in the conservatory parking lot and made it clear that the news about his alleged misconduct had already spread.

Perhaps his reaction was that of an innocent man. Abby always tried to follow her instincts, but this case had her spinning in all different directions. Mick was right, though. Until they had more proof, they couldn't accuse anyone of the crimes perpetrated against the orcas.

So she'd have to find that proof.

CHAPTER ❦ NINETEEN

ABBY AND TESSA TOOK the ferry from Green Harbor over to Lopez Island. The day was cloudy and overcast, making Abby wish she'd brought a jacket with her for the journey. Tessa stood beside her on the ferry, her face creased with anxiety.

"I hope he'll be happy to see me," Tessa said. "I probably should have had my hair done first." She held out her hands, frowning down at them. "And gotten a manicure. Just look at my nails."

"Your hair and your nails both look fine," Abby told her. "Try to relax."

Tessa didn't exactly relax on the rest of the journey, but she did let herself be distracted by the birds Abby pointed out along the way. They saw a black oystercatcher, a spotted sandpiper and a pair of playful harlequin ducks.

"What does Marshall look like now?" Tessa asked wistfully. "Still tall, I'm sure. But is he as thin as a rail or heavy? Does he have all his thick brown hair or has he lost some of it? I don't suppose he still wears cowboy boots, does he? I got him a pair as a gift for his birthday right before we left for Ohio. Marshall told me that he'd wear them forever."

Abby smiled at the long litany of questions, hearing Tessa's own insecurities in her voice. "He's not too thin or too heavy," she told her. "In fact, I'd say he's just about right. His hair is still brown, though with enough gray mixed in to make him look quite distinguished. He has a beard, too."

"A beard?" Tessa exclaimed, then laughed. "Are you serious? I can't imagine what he must look like with a beard."

Abby smiled, feeling a little nervous herself now. Marshall and Tessa had been apart for such a long time. She hoped this reunion would be a blessing to both of them.

Tessa tilted her face up to the sky. "I'd forgotten how beautiful it is here. How peaceful it makes me feel. I'm not sure the sky is this blue in Ohio. Or maybe I just never bothered to really look at it."

Abby knew exactly what she meant. When she'd returned to the San Juan Islands after Mary's accident, she'd been affected the same way. It still struck her once in a while even now, the awesome power of God's creation that was always right in front of her.

When they landed on Lopez Island, Abby and Tessa walked from the dock to Marshall's shop in the village. But to Abby's surprise, The Woodchuck's Den was closed.

"He's probably at his house," Abby said, aware that it was too long a journey to make by foot, especially since most of it was uphill. Abby might be up for the hike, but she knew Tessa wouldn't want to arrive all winded and sweaty.

So they took a taxi, Tessa insisting on paying the entire fare, to make the trip to Marshall's house. Abby gave directions to the taxi driver, then they settled into the backseat.

"How long have you lived on Sparrow Island?" Tessa asked her.

"I grew up there," Abby explained. "But I moved to New York and taught at Cornell University. I was gone for a long time—close to thirty-five years."

"Even longer than me," Tessa mused. "Funny how this place still feels like home."

As the taxi climbed up the steep drive leading to Marshall's house, Abby saw Tessa's grip tighten on the door handle.

"Are you okay?" Abby asked her.

Tessa took a deep breath, then exhaled slowly. "I think so. It's hard to explain, I feel excited and terrified at the same time. Does that sound completely crazy to you?"

"No," Abby assured her as the taxi slowed to a stop. "Not crazy at all. I'd be worried if you weren't excited and terrified."

Tessa nodded, two bright pink spots in her cheeks. "Okay, then. I guess this is it."

Abby smiled, her heart going out to the woman. This day had been thirty years in coming; it was no wonder she was so nervous.

As they climbed out of the car, Tessa paid the driver, then turned to Abby. "Would you mind going to the door first, just to give Marshall some warning?"

"Not at all," Abby replied, moving toward the house. She ascended the porch steps with Tessa just a few feet behind her. Then Tessa moved off to the side while Abby knocked on the door.

When there was no answer, she knocked again. She had

seen his car in the driveway so she knew Marshall wouldn't be too far away.

At last Abby heard footsteps and breathed a sigh of relief. A moment later the door opened and Marshall stood on the other side.

"Well, this is a nice surprise," he said, his mouth curving into a smile when he saw her. "Sorry I took so long, I've been doing some painting and was washing up when you knocked."

She could see flecks of white paint on his faded chambray work shirt and denim jeans. A glance down toward his feet revealed a pair of worn brown cowboy boots with a splatter of white paint on them.

Tessa's boots? It seemed impossible after thirty years, but Abby wasn't going to rule anything out after the twists and turns this romance had taken.

"Are you ready for another surprise?" Abby asked him, hoping he liked surprises. "Because I brought someone to see you."

"You did?" His face crinkled in bewilderment, Marshall stepped outside.

Tessa stood in the glow of the sun, her blonde hair gleaming like spun gold and her forty-seven-year-old face shining with hope.

Marshall's mouth fell open when he saw her. He was completely speechless.

Tessa swallowed hard, gathering her courage. "Hello, Marshall."

"Tessa," he whispered, still staring at her in shock. "Is it really you?"

"Yes, it's really me." She reached up to nervously comb her fingers through the ends of her hair. "I know you weren't expecting me. I should have called first. I hope this isn't a bad time."

Abby resisted the urge to grab them each by the hand and pull them together. But she knew they had to do this in their own way and in their own time. She took a step back, though neither seemed to notice her presence.

"No, this isn't a bad time at all," Marshall insisted, then he looked down at his clothes. He blushed beneath his beard. "I'm not exactly dressed for company."

Tessa took a step toward him. "I think you look . . . amazing."

His gaze caressed her face as he moved toward her. "You look exactly the same, Tessa. You haven't a changed a bit."

She laughed at his words and the sound crumpled the wall of politeness between them. He slowly reached out and touched her hand. Her small fingers curled around his large palm, then she looked up into his eyes.

The next moment, they were in each others arms.

Abby stepped off the porch, giving the two of them a private moment. This was better than any of those romantic movies she and Mary liked to watch. Tessa and Marshall truly deserved their happily ever after.

Abby strolled over to the edge of the cliff, looking out onto the water. Mick's boat was still anchored out there, and she could see a few members of his crew walking on the deck.

Several minutes later, Marshall and Tessa joined her there, walking hand-in-hand. Neither one of them could stop smiling.

"Thank you," Marshall said. "Thank you for bringing my Tessa to me."

"It was my pleasure," Abby assured him.

Marshall circled his arm around Tessa's waist as she looked in wonder at the beauty of nature that surrounded them.

"This view is breathtaking," Tessa exclaimed. "How could I have stayed away from here for so long?"

Marshall gazed down at his beloved with hope shining in his brown eyes. "Does that mean you plan to stay awhile?"

"I'm scheduled to fly back to my new place in Boston today," Tessa answered, "but I think I'll cancel my flight."

He smiled at her words. "We'll fly our pigeons instead. I've built a new loft since you've been gone. And I can't wait to introduce you to some of Harold's descendents."

Abby looked at him. "Harold has chicks already?"

Marshall laughed. "The Harold you found is actually Harold the fifth."

"Dover is his great, great grandmother, the pigeon I took with me when I moved to Ohio thirty years ago," Tessa explained. "Her descendants have been making the journey between our two homes ever since."

The sound of loud rock music echoed off the water, making them all look toward Mick's boat.

Marshall shook his head in disgust. "I'll sure be glad when that guy finds someplace else to anchor his boat. That music keeps me awake all night long."

"Mick and his crew are all young men," Abby replied. "They probably keep late hours."

"That they do," Marshall confirmed. "But it's how they act during the day that I can't figure out."

"What do you mean?" Abby asked him.

"Well, I'm used to seeing boats taking fish out of the water, but for about the last two weeks the crew from this boat has been throwing fish *into* the water."

"That is strange," Tessa agreed. "Why would they do that?"

Marshall shrugged. "Who knows? Maybe they catch more than they can eat."

"Or maybe," Abby said, her mind whirling, "the fish isn't for them to eat at all."

She stepped closer to the edge, squinting her gaze at Mick's boat in the distance. But she was too far out to see anything clearly.

"Marshall," she said, her instincts kicking in again. "Do you have a pair of binoculars I can borrow?"

CHAPTER ❦ TWENTY

STILL REELING FROM HER discovery on Lopez Island, Abby returned to the conservatory to plan her next move. She walked into her office at The Nature Museum and slipped on her lab coat. The double-crested cormorant chicks would need to be fed soon.

As she checked the rest of her schedule, Abby found she couldn't concentrate. Not after what she'd seen from that cliff. She didn't want to act too hastily, but time was of the essence.

Before Abby could decide anything, Hugo burst into her office.

"I have some wonderful news!" he exclaimed. "The orca calf has been found."

"What?" Abby cried, caught off guard by this latest turn of events.

"Isn't it fantastic?" Hugo couldn't stop smiling. "Poppy's alive and well. Mick found her and is taking her back to the K pod as we speak. Then he's holding a press conference here in one hour."

Abby took a moment to process everything Hugo was saying. "Where did Mick find Poppy?"

"Somewhere near Lopez Island," Hugo told her. "It was a very short phone call, so I didn't get all the details. He should be here soon to set up for the press conference, so you can ask him then. That young man is going to be a hero."

A hero.

His words made everything fall into place for Abby. She hadn't wanted to believe it, but this was more than a coincidence.

Hugo's smile faded as he took in Abby's expression. "Is something wrong, Abby? I thought you'd be happier about this news."

"I'm thrilled about it," she replied honestly. The weeks of worry about the missing orca calf were finally over. "I just have so many things on my mind right now."

"Well, I'll make certain everything is ready to go for the press conference." He rubbed his hands together. "We're going to hold it in the workroom, but not let the press inside until right before it starts. Mick believes that will help build the suspense."

Her phone rang before Abby could reply.

"Go ahead and take that call," Hugo said, heading toward the door. "I've got quite a few things to get ready. Will I see you at the press conference?"

"I'll be there," Abby promised as the phone rang a second time.

She picked up the receiver. "Hello?"

"Abby, is that you?"

She recognized the voice on the other end of the line and joy shot through her. "Lauren?"

"Yes, it's me," Lauren Sima replied. "How are you? It's so great to hear your voice again. I've really missed you."

"I'm good," Abby said, leaning against her desk. Lauren had perfect timing. She desperately needed someone to confide in. "And I've missed you, too. But I love living back home, Lauren, more than I ever imagined."

"I'm so glad," Lauren replied. "Unlike you, I seem to have caught a travel bug. I just can't stop globe-trotting."

Abby laughed. "Speaking of travel, how was your trip to Greece?"

"Absolutely amazing," Lauren said. "I'm planning to go back there over Christmas break. I hope you'll consider joining me."

"I'll think about it," Abby promised, her current dilemma distracting her from the conversation. She checked her watch, wondering how much time she had until Mick's press conference.

"Okay, spill it," Lauren said, before Abby even had a chance to broach a new subject. "You know I can always tell when something's wrong."

Abby smiled into the phone. Despite Lauren's blunt manner, they were kindred spirits. They'd always been able to read each other's moods.

"I met Mick Wymore recently."

"Ah," Lauren replied. "That explains it. Where did you meet him?"

Her response surprised Abby. She sounded less than enthusiastic about him. Yet, Mick had made Abby think that Lauren was one of his biggest fans.

"He's doing his doctoral research in the San Juan Islands," Abby said. "He just arrived here a few weeks ago."

"His doctoral research?" Lauren echoed in surprise. "How is

that possible when he dropped out of the master's program here?"

Abby sank into her office chair. "Oh no."

"Oh yes," Lauren countered. "Look, I think Mick wants to be successful, he just doesn't want to have to work very hard for it. He's handsome and charming with a great personality. That's the problem. He's gotten by on his looks and his people skills for far too long."

"He's very outgoing," Abby agreed. "Everybody here loves him. He fit in right away. Now it's almost like he's a local celebrity."

Lauren sighed. "That doesn't surprise me at all. Mick can win over people with so little effort that he starts to believe all the hype about himself. I'm sorry to say that the Mick Wymore I know is all show and no substance."

"He does seem to like the spotlight."

"He lives for it," Lauren said bluntly. "I've always believed that it's going to catch up with him some day. And his fall is going to be a hard one."

Abby remembered Mick's arrival at the conservatory and how he'd misrepresented himself from the first day. Even telling her that Lauren had asked him to say hello for her, when her friend hadn't even known he'd been coming.

Had he just been trying to get in Abby's good graces or was there another reason? Maybe the man was so used to lying he didn't know how to do anything else.

"I think that day may be here, Lauren." She twisted the phone cord in her hand. "I have reason to believe he's involved in a crime."

Lauren didn't say anything for a moment. "Then you have to do something about it, Abby."

Once again, her friend had sensed Abby's mood and her reluctance to go forward. "Mick seemed so nice at first, Lauren. So ready to do anything he could to help out. That's what makes this so hard."

"I know," Lauren said, her tone gentler now. "But that's Mick's modus operandi. He likes to make a big splash but leaves it to everyone else to clean up the mess."

Abby couldn't argue with that assessment. Mick had promised to help look for the missing orca calf, but she didn't have any proof that he'd done anything more than hold press conferences and organize that candlelight vigil—events that put him in the spotlight.

For a man who claimed to have a burning passion to study the social and familial relationships in orca pods, he hadn't once talked about observing a pod.

He'd probably been too busy granting interviews and talking about movie deals and negotiating with his agent. Then again, if he didn't have a master's degree, he couldn't be working on his doctorate.

Which meant he'd lied to Abby from the start.

"If you care about Mick," Lauren continued, "then you know you can't let him get away with anything. If that young man's ever going to amount to something, if he's ever going to fulfill the great potential that God has blessed him with, then he needs to be held accountable for his actions."

That was another reason Abby liked her friend Lauren so much. She let her deep and abiding faith guide her through life. Abby always tried to do the same, especially when faced with a difficult situation such as the one before her now.

Abby had a feeling that Mick had done more than rescue the orca calf. She believed that he'd kidnapped Poppy and held her in captivity until just the right moment. The view she'd seen through Marshall's binoculars had shown her a large net stretched from the bow of the boat into the water. She'd seen the orca calf inside that net breaching the surface as Mick's crew had thrown fish overboard.

Mick might very well try to convince her and everyone else that he'd just found Poppy today, but the evidence to the contrary was too overwhelming. Marshall had seen the crew dump fish into the water every day for more than two weeks. The boat had never moved, anchoring in a secluded cove where no other vessels ventured near enough to catch sight of the captive Poppy.

She still didn't know why Mick had chosen today to announce the dramatic rescue. Perhaps he had sensed the story waning in the press. Or he feared the experts wouldn't believe that the orca calf could survive any longer on her own. More likely, he somehow knew Abby was on to him and wanted to take the offensive before he was caught red-handed.

"Thank you, Lauren," Abby told her friend, grateful for her timely phone call. "I appreciate everything you've told me."

"I hope it all works out, Abby."

"So do I," she said, then checked her watch. "I'd better go now."

"All right, I'll be praying for you," Lauren promised. "and for Mick."

"I'll talk to you soon," Abby said, then hung up the phone.

Her hand rested on the receiver as she contemplated her next move. She'd been about to call Henry and tell him her suspicions before Hugo had burst into her office. But the press conference was due to start soon and she needed to act fast.

Once Mick announced his dramatic rescue of the orca calf,

the press would make him an instant hero. Any claims Abby made afterward might be drowned out in the ensuing media blitz. Some of Mick's fans, people who knew she'd been investigating the case, might even say her accusation against him was sour grapes.

But Abby couldn't let that possibility concern her. She wasn't doing this for accolades, only to see justice done. Which meant she had to prove Mick was guilty before he used the press conference to obscure the facts of the case.

Now was her only chance. Abby couldn't let this charade continue any longer. She had to confront Mick and make him confess the truth.

No matter what it took.

Abby found Mick alone in the workroom. He was moving the wooden podium in front of several rows of folding chairs that had been set up for the reporters. The shadow of whiskers on his jaw gave him a rugged appearance, accented even more by the green pea coat he wore over a black turtleneck and matching black pants.

A man ready to face the cameras.

A man ready to be a hero.

"Hello, Abby," he said, sliding the podium into place. "I see you're here for the big announcement."

She noticed that he'd gotten a haircut since the last time she'd seen him. Styling gel separated each strand, curling the blond hair at his neck and making him look more like a dashing movie star than ever.

"I wouldn't miss it," she said, hearing the murmur of voices outside the double doors of the workroom. Members of the press had started to arrive. She knew the television crews would want to enter soon to set up their lights and cameras.

Mick rubbed his hands together. "Well, we got our happy

ending, Abby. Poppy has been happily reunited with the K pod and is swimming with her mother as we speak."

"I'm glad to hear it," she replied. "I'm sure your agent will be thrilled by the news, too."

Mick nodded. "I already called him. He says that Poppy's rescue should double the offers for the story. Better buy a new dress for the movie premiere."

Buoyed by the prospect of money and fame, Mick was becoming obnoxious about it. She wondered if he'd always been that way and just hidden it well or if the limelight had really gone to his head.

Abby watched him brush a speck of lint off his pea coat as the voices of the press grew louder out in the hallway. She didn't have much time left.

"You've been busy," Abby said, ready to follow Henry's advice and let Mick incriminate himself.

He nodded, shuffling his notes on the podium in front of him. "This is a very big day. For the San Juan Islands, I mean. And the Sparrow Island Nature Conservatory. We've got news people coming here from all over. I think this story could go international."

"Mick," Abby said, waiting until she had his attention before she continued. "I saw your boat this afternoon."

He blinked, confusion etched in his face. "What?"

"I saw your boat anchored in a secluded cove off Lopez Island a few hours ago. I was visiting a friend of mine there."

He hesitated, as if uncertain what to say next. "Yes, that's a beautiful area."

"Private, too," Abby said. "Not too many boaters go out there."

"That's why I chose it."

"For the privacy?" Abby asked. "Or because you were keeping something out there that you didn't want anyone else to see?"

His eyes met hers and in that moment Abby knew she was right. Disappointment seeped through her. She had wanted to be wrong about him.

"Why, Mick?" she asked.

His nostrils flared. "I don't know what you're talking about."

"I think you do. My friend said your crew has been throwing fish into the water for the last couple of weeks. There's only one reason to do that, isn't there?"

His gaze narrowed on her. "Look, Abby, this really isn't the time or the place to talk about it. Maybe we can go out for dinner sometime in the next few days. After all the publicity has died down."

"But you're not going to let that happen, are you, Mick?" She moved closer to him, observing the sheen of perspiration on his brow. "You've got an agent now and a movie deal in the works. All thanks to the orca calf. Poppy's going to make you famous."

A muscle in his jaw twitched as he mulled over her words. "I didn't do anything to that orca calf. Poppy's fine. Certainly better than she was when she strayed from the K pod. She might very well be dead right now if it wasn't for me."

Abby could see the guilt in his blue eyes. That was the reason he was trying to rationalize his behavior. She knew he was close to telling her the truth. "When did you find her? Or was she never really lost?"

He opened his mouth to respond, then closed it again. His gaze moved past Abby to the door behind her.

She turned to see Captain Hovel entering the room.

"Hello, Lew," Mick said with a sigh of relief. "You're just in time."

CHAPTER ❦ TWENTY-ONE

Hᴏᴡ ᴅɪᴅ ʏᴏᴜ ɢᴇᴛ ɪɴ here?" Abby asked Captain Hovel.

He leaned against the closed door and folded his arms across his chest, a snide smile curving his mouth. "I'm one of the speakers for the press conference. Mick asked me to give my perspective of the story as a seasoned whale-watch tour boat operator."

Mick rounded the podium. "She knows what we did, Lew. She knows everything."

Abby looked between the two of them and the disappointment she'd felt earlier morphed into anger. "So you two are in this together?"

Hovel scowled at Mick. "Shut up, kid. Dr. Stanton doesn't *know* anything."

Now it all made sense. Mick hadn't come upon the lost orca calf accidentally, the entire event had been staged. He and Hovel had been working in tandem from the beginning, each for their own gain. That's why Mick had been so quick to defend Captain Hovel and try to shift her attention to other suspects—first the Andersons, then Captain Zirka.

"I know you used *The Sea Prince* to sail through the K pod," Abby countered, not about to let Captain Hovel bully her. "I'm sure the reporters will be interested to hear what Judd Peavey has to say about your involvement."

Captain Hovel shrugged, looking unconcerned. "His word against mine."

"It's not supposed to be like this," Mick muttered, looking more flustered by the minute.

Abby stared at Mick, wondering if he could really be that naïve. "Whose idea was it to sail through the K pod in the first place, Mick? Yours or Captain Hovel's?"

"Don't say a word, kid," Hovel growled.

But Abby could see the disillusionment in Mick's blue eyes. The dreams of glory he'd built up for himself were starting to crumble.

"It was Captain Hovel's idea, wasn't it?" Abby said to Mick. "He talked you into it."

Hovel took a menacing step toward Abby. "That's enough," he warned.

But Mick saw an escape route in her words and started scrambling toward it. "Yes, it was all his idea. I met him years ago, when we both lived in Maine. He's the one who talked me into coming here after I left Cornell."

"Why here?" Abby asked, though she already knew the answer. Hovel had been plotting this for a long time.

"Because he said the orca researchers here were always looking for extra help." His face darkened. "But the scientists at The Whale Museum didn't want anything to do with me because I didn't have some hoity-toity graduate degree. That's when Hovel told me he knew a way I could have everything I wanted."

"You're an idiot," Captain Hovel cried, giving Mick a shove.

Mick stumbled back, but kept his balance. Now that he'd started talking, he wasn't going to stop. "You're the idiot, Lew, thinking that we could ever get away with something like this. You've made one stupid mistake after another."

Mick shook his head in disgust as he continued his diatribe. "First, using a bunch of hired sailors who we couldn't trust to keep their mouths shut. Then trying to make yourself the hero by rescuing the people from *The Sea Prince*—a boat that you made sure was going to sink that day."

Now all the pieces of the puzzle started to fall together for Abby. "You were the scuba diver," she said, facing Captain Hovel. "You deliberately scuttled *The Sea Prince* so it would go down. That's why *The Adventurer* was in the area, wasn't it? So we'd be close enough to see that *The Sea Prince* was in distress."

"That's right," Mick insisted, his face flushed. "Except he hired someone to do that part of the job as well. He was starting to feel the heat of your investigation and wanted to put the blame squarely on Zirka. He knew if *The Sea Prince* started to founder, help would be there soon enough to tow it back to shore. Then it could be dry-docked and there would be solid evidence that it was the boat that rammed the mother orca."

Hovel grabbed him by the shoulders and shook him. "Will you shut up already? Don't you see what she's trying to do here? Dr. Stanton doesn't have any solid proof against either of us. She's just trying to goad you into confessing everything."

Mick blinked as if this realization hadn't occurred to him. "But *I* didn't really do anything wrong."

"Really?" Captain Hovel scoffed. "Then why did you race out

to kidnap the orca calf as soon as the McDonald kid showed you that picture? You had Poppy in your net before sundown."

Her hope that Mick had come upon the orca calf accidentally died with Captain Hovel's words. Now Abby knew that Mick had not only schemed and collaborated with Captain Hovel to disrupt the K pod, but had kidnapped the orca calf at the first opportunity. No doubt to take advantage of the situation for all it was worth.

And if Abby hadn't figured out their plan, it would have been worth a lot. With Mick's talent at charming people, he would have made a fortune in personal appearances and speaking engagements, not to mention his pending movie deal. Captain Hovel probably knew it, too, and had been planning to take a big cut of the rewards.

The pallor on Mick's face told her he knew those golden opportunities were starting to slip through his fingers.

"There's only one thing to do," Captain Hovel said, still holding Mick's shoulders in his firm grasp. "We shut her up. Keep her out of sight long enough to make our announcement, then get out of here."

Mick stared at him. "And just how are we going to do that?"

"Same way I did with Zirka," Hovel replied. "Tie her up, hide her in my boat for a while, then drop her off hundreds of miles from here. By the time she makes it back, we'll both be long gone."

So Captain Dennis Zirka hadn't run off after selling his boat, he'd been abducted. Abby suppressed a shiver at the sheer disregard for life, human or animal, that Captain Hovel displayed.

"Captain Zirka knew what you did," Abby said, facing Lewis Hovel. "Is that why you had to get rid of him? To keep your dirty secret?"

Captain Hovel rolled his eyes. "He was a drunk. Chances are that wherever he is now, he doesn't even remember what happened that night."

"Now wait a minute." Mick raked a hand through his perfectly styled hair. "Let's think this through, Lew. How do we get her out of here and onto your boat without anybody noticing? The hallway out there is full of reporters."

Abby watched Hovel pull a small gun from his pocket, then she stepped back in horror. All the blood drained from Mick's face as he gaped at his accomplice.

"She'll go with us nice and quiet," he said with a creepy smile. "Won't you, Dr. Stanton?"

Before she could reply, one of the double doors opened and Bobby walked inside. Hovel slipped his gun in his jacket pocket before the boy could see it, though the bulge it made against the tweed fabric still pointed in Abby's direction.

Her heart dropped to her toes, more out of fear for Bobby than for herself. Lewis Hovel was a desperate man who showed no regard for anyone or anything. Something told her he wouldn't let a child stand in the way of his plans either.

"Hey," Bobby said, unaware of the tension between the three of them. "I'm supposed to ask you if we can let the reporters in here yet."

"Get rid of him," Hovel told Abby in a harsh whisper. "Now."

This was her one chance. It was obvious that Hovel and Mick weren't going to let her leave on her own. Not when she knew too much about their nefarious operations.

"*Snickerdoodles*," Abby said, looking straight at Bobby and hoping he comprehended her secret message.

"What?" Bobby said, then understanding dawned on his face. "You want *snickerdoodles*?"

"Yes, I do," she said, giving him a slight nod, "to serve to the reporters after the press conference. "Please get some *snickerdoodles* as fast as you can. Hugo should know where to look."

Without another word, the boy turned and raced out of the room. Abby breathed a sigh of relief. She sent up a silent prayer to thank God for keeping Bobby safe from harm.

Hovel scowled in her direction. "What was that all about?"

"Bobby loves snickerdoodles," Abby said truthfully. "I knew just saying the word would get him to leave. That's what you wanted, wasn't it?"

"Who cares about some stupid snickerdoodles?" Mick fumed, starting to pace. "We've got to figure out how to get out of this mess."

Abby's mind whirled as she considered what to do if Captain Hovel tried to take her from the conservatory at gunpoint. She didn't want to go willingly, but if she put up a struggle, that might put other lives at risk.

"I've already figured it out." Captain Hovel grabbed her arm and started pulling her toward the double doors. "Come on, let's go."

"Wait," Mick said, blocking his path, "this is crazy. That hallway's full of reporters. Besides, you're not actually considering *shooting* her, are you?"

Hovel frowned at him. "Then what do you suggest, genius?"

Mick looked around the room, then pointed at the window. "We could go out that way—cut our losses."

Hovel shook his head. "Dumb idea, college boy. She'll raise the alarm so fast, we won't even make it to the parking lot."

Mick wrung his hands together. "Look I went into this for some publicity. I'm no killer."

Hovel pointed the gun at Mick. "She's going into the closet and you're going to give the best press conference of your life. Understand?"

Abby could see that Mick was in way over his head. "You'd better do what he says."

Hovel steered her toward the closet. "I'll stand guard right outside this closet door. If Dr. Stanton does cause any kind of disturbance it will be the last noise she ever makes."

Her mind raced to come up with an idea to thwart his plan. She couldn't let him get away with this, but she was no match against that gun.

Mick followed them over to the closet, looking even more scared than Abby. "Wait, I—"

"I need something to gag her with," Hovel interjected. He gave Abby a shove into the closet, then reached for the handkerchief sticking out of Mick's pocket.

That's when she saw the walking stick Marshall had given her.

It was thick and sturdy, solid wood, at least three inches in diameter. Before they could react, she picked it up and shoved it in Hovel's belly. He let out a grunt of pain, dropping the gun.

Abby pushed him into Mick, causing both men to lose their balance and fall to the floor. She took advantage of the opportunity to run for the double doors that led to the hallway, the walking stick still in her hands.

She heard footsteps pounding behind her, but made it through the doors first. Then she stuck the thick walking stick through the handles right before the hard thud of a man's body hit the doors.

The walking stick held against the impact, preventing the doors from opening. Reporters began to gather around Abby, lobbing questions at her about all the commotion inside the workroom.

"What's going on?" they called out to her, their camera lights flashing. "Who's in there?"

"Call the police," she shouted, trying to make her way through the crowd.

Hugo ran up to her, grasping her by the shoulders. "The police are already on their way. Bobby told us you sent him for help. What happened in there? Are you all right?"

She had to take a moment to catch her breath. "Captain Hovel is the one who deliberately sailed through the orca pod. Mick was involved, too. He was keeping the orca calf captive."

Hugo's eyes widened in shock. "What?"

"It's true," she told him. "I still don't understand why Mick would do something so heinous."

Despite the uproar in the hallway, there was now an eerie silence coming from the workroom. Abby knew the two men would look for some means of escape now that she was free to tell everything she knew.

"The window," she exclaimed, pulling out of Hugo's grasp. "We can't let them get away!"

They rushed out the front entrance, the reporters in hot pursuit. Rounding the building, they saw that Captain Hovel lay writhing on the ground beneath the open window, holding onto his ankle.

Mick was in the parking lot, his path blocked by Sergeant Henry Cobb's car. He raised his hands up in the air to surrender.

The publicity Mick had desired so much swung into action

as reporters ran onto the scene. They started shouting questions at Captain Hovel as he lay hurt on the ground.

Henry handcuffed Mick, then marched him over to Hugo and Abby. "Looks like I got here just in time."

Mick hung his head, ignoring the questions of reporters and their cameras. His yearning for the spotlight had obviously waned.

Bobby appeared out of the crowd and ran toward Abby. When he reached her, she gave him a big hug. "Thank you for figuring out my secret message. You saved the day."

"Hey, it was an easy one," he replied, blushing at the compliment. "Anybody could figure it out as long as you know the code."

"What code?" Henry asked, looking between the two of them.

Abby smiled, exchanging glances with her young neighbor. "Bobby and I have a secret code word in case either one of us ever needs help."

"What is it?" Henry asked, looking impressed by their ingenuity.

"Snickerdoodles," Bobby told him.

Mick looked up in dismay. "Snickerdoodles? That's how the kid knew to the call the police? *Snickerdoodles?*"

"That's right," Abby replied. "Snickerdoodles is our new way of asking for emergency assistance. Right, Bobby?"

"Right," he affirmed. "They taste good, too."

After Henry placed Mick in his squad car, he approached Abby again. "Are you sure you're all right, Abby? That was quite a collar you just made."

"I'm fine," she said, although she still felt a little shaky.

"Well, as soon as you're ready I'll need to take your statement, although Mr. Wymore is already trying to make a deal. He told me about his involvement with Lewis Hovel and what happened in the workroom."

Captain Hovel overheard Henry and looked up, his expression mingled with pain and rage. "Don't believe a word Mick Wymore says! They're just trying to frame me. It's my word against his." He jabbed a finger in Abby's direction. "And my word against hers."

"Don't worry, Captain." Abby pulled the microcassette recorder from the pocket of her lab coat, the voice-activated tape still running. "I'll let this do all the talking for you."

His mouth dropped open in surprise, then his shoulders sagged. He couldn't claim his innocence anymore, not when she had his own words on tape to incriminate him.

An ambulance arrived and after the paramedics set his broken ankle, they carefully loaded Hovel onto the stretcher. He pulled the lapel of his jacket over his face to shield himself from all the cameras.

Mick did the same as Henry drove him away in the squad car. Abby still couldn't believe that he'd been a willing participant in Lewis Hovel's scheme.

"I'm still in shock," Hugo said, watching Henry's squad car leave the parking lot, "and very disappointed in that young man."

Abby knew Hugo's shock and disappointment would only grow when he heard the full story. "Mick fooled everyone."

The reporters scampered toward the vehicles, ready to follow the story. When it hit the news, Mick Wymore would get more publicity than he ever imagined.

CHAPTER 🌹 TWENTY-TWO

ABBY ARRIVED AT THE sheriff's substation the next day to give Henry her full statement. She'd already handed over the microcassette tape, so he only needed her to fill in a few of the blanks.

His face grew grim when she got to the part about Hovel pulling a gun on her. As she related the details, it almost seemed to Abby as if it had happened in a dream. She knew that traumatic events sometimes took a few days to sink in. Rev. Hale had already contacted her and offered to be available any time if she wanted to talk to him.

Abby appreciated his concern, but she'd been talking to God since the incident happened and knew she'd be all right.

She hoped the same would be true for the orca calf. Despite Mick's assurance that Poppy was healthy and reunited with her mother, Abby hoped the stress of captivity hadn't harmed the orca calf in any way.

Henry closed the folder in front of him. "I think that's about all I need. I'll give you a call if I have any more questions."

Abby stood up. "Thank you, Henry. Will I see you at the house sometime soon?"

He nodded. "I still need to give Mary her jewelry box, but I'd like to put a bracelet or necklace or something in it first. I just haven't been able to find exactly the right piece of jewelry."

Abby smiled, certain her sister would be thrilled with the gift no matter when he chose to give it to her. "As it happens, the man who made that jewelry box makes beautiful jewelry too. He has a shop on Lopez Island called The Woodchuck's Den."

Henry looked up at her in surprise. "I've seen that place, but I've never stopped in there."

"He's got beautiful wooden pendants and bracelets with intricate carvings. I'm sure you could find something unique that Mary would love."

"Great idea, Abby," he said, rising to his feet. "I'll stop by there after work today."

"I can't wait to see what you pick out," she said as she headed toward the door.

"Abby," he said as she reached for the door handle, "there's one more thing. Mr. Wymore wants to see you."

She turned around to face him, surprised by the request. After their last encounter, Abby had assumed Mick would never want to see her again. "Are you sure about that?"

Henry nodded. "You certainly don't have to agree to see him, especially after what he and Hovel put you through. The choice is yours."

Abby knew that if she refused, she'd always wonder about what Mick wanted to say to her. Besides, she was still curious about the reason he'd gotten involved with Captain Hovel's scheme in the first place. There had to be more to it than his love of the limelight.

"I'll see him," she told Henry.

Five minutes later, she found herself in a small interview room, seated across a table from Mick. He wore an orange prison jumpsuit and a dour expression. Henry stood in the doorway.

"Are you sure you'll be all right in here?" Henry asked her. "I'll be happy to stay."

"She'll be fine," Mick promised him. "I'm not going to hurt her."

Abby swallowed a sigh at his words. What Mick obviously didn't realize was that he'd already hurt her. Just like he'd hurt all the people who had believed in him and his mission to save the orca calf. None of them had realized he'd orchestrated the whole thing from the very beginning. They had all put their trust in Mick, only to be disappointed.

After Henry left, Mick turned to face her. "I know what you must think of me."

"You do?"

He nodded. "But you just don't understand. I didn't really do anything wrong."

Abby stared at him in amazement. Either Mick was in complete denial or he was trying to con her again. "You conspired with Captain Hovel to sail through the orca pod. The mother orca was injured and almost died. Poppy was separated from her family for almost three weeks. How can you say you did nothing wrong?"

His mouth turned down in a mulish frown. "I never told Hovel to hit the mother orca. I just wanted him to stir things up a little around here."

"So you could step in and play the hero?"

"I just wanted to be famous, you know? I never wanted to hurt anybody or anything. I love orcas. I love all animals."

Abby shook her head. "Surely there are easier ways of becoming famous. Legal ways."

Frustration filled his face. "I didn't want to have to spend the next few decades trying to prove myself. I'm already twenty-five years old. And I know whales better than anyone, even those experts at The Whale Museum."

Mick buried his head in his hands. "The orcas are becoming an endangered species and needed a voice. I just wanted to be that voice. Is that so wrong?"

He just doesn't get it. Abby wondered if he ever would.

"Yes, Mick it is wrong," she said softly. "Because you used lies and deception to try and reach your goal. You put the orcas in danger, the very creatures you now claim you want to save."

He looked up at her. "I never meant it to go as far as it did. I just got caught up in all the drama. That first press conference was so incredible. Everybody was listening to me and the story started to take on a life of its own."

"And you liked the spotlight."

He lifted his chin in defiance. "I was born for it, Abby. When I captured the baby orca, I was thrilled at first. Then I thought about how quickly the whole thing would be over. I mean, the story was just starting to build. We were starting to get national exposure."

"So you decided to keep Poppy under wraps for a while so you could build the momentum."

"Exactly." He sighed. "I figured it couldn't hurt and it might even help the conservatory and The Nature Museum, as well as make people more aware of the delicate marine ecosystems."

But Abby wasn't about to let Mick continue to make excuses for his behavior. "Keeping Poppy away from her family, away from the K pod, was cruel. You can't justify it, Mick."

"I just wanted some glory," he said, his mouth turning down in a petulant frown. "I've been working hard, putting myself through college. I deserve something for it."

"Glory belongs to God," she told him. "Not to men. Look where your quest for glory has led you."

His gaze dropped to his wrists, which were handcuffed together on the table. Then he slumped back in his chair, his shoulders sagging.

Abby sensed that there was nothing more she could say that would get through to him today. No doubt he'd have plenty of time to think about it. Perhaps in the future, as he grew older and wiser, he'd see the error of his ways.

Without another word, she rose from her chair and left the room, praying that Mick would someday find the right path in life.

Henry met her by the front desk. "There are several serious charges pending against both Captain Hovel and Mick Wymore. I don't think either one of them will ever bother you again."

"I'm just glad it's over," Abby replied, eager to put the whole thing behind her.

Henry nodded. "Poppy took the long way home, but she's finally back with her family in the K pod now. Thanks to you."

Home. That was exactly where Abby wanted to be.

THE FOLLOWING MONDAY, everything was back to normal on Sparrow Island. Abby sat at the desk in her office, updating her computer records when Hugo knocked on the open door.

"May I come in?" he asked, looking as dapper as ever in his charcoal gray suit.

"Please do," Abby replied, setting down her pen. "I could

use a distraction from all this paperwork. I know it needs to be done, but I can't help but notice the beautiful day outside."

He walked into her office and took a seat across from her desk. "I just got off the telephone with Henry Cobb. He told me that Mick Wymore and Lewis Hovel have both signed plea agreements admitting their guilt in the orca case. So there won't be a court trial."

Relief swept through Abby. That meant there wouldn't be any more publicity about the incident and everyone could finally put it behind them. "Will they both be going to jail?"

Hugo nodded. "Mick will spend a few months there, enough time to make him realize the seriousness of his offenses. Lewis Hovel pled guilty to much more serious charges, including his abduction of Captain Zirka and the fact that he pulled a gun on you."

"Then it's finally over," Abby murmured. "Hopefully, nothing like this will ever happen again."

"I think everyone around here will be much more conscientious about the fragility of the orca pods and their environment," Hugo said. "The good news is that Poppy is active and fully integrated back into the K pod. The scientists at The Whale Museum have given her a clean bill of health."

Abby smiled. "That's good news. I know the Andersons will be happy to hear it. They've just bought a new boat with their insurance money from *The Luna* and are launching it in Poppy's honor tomorrow."

Hugo looked surprised. "I thought they were going to retire."

"So did I," Abby replied, "but Margie Anderson told me when they sat down and talked about how they wanted to spend their retirement years, they both wanted to be on the water educating people about the orcas."

"Good for them." Hugo stood up. "What about *The Sea Prince*?"

"It's undergoing repairs and should be as good as new," Abby told him. "Kyle Breslin is determined to make North Star Cruises the top touring line in the San Juan Islands."

Hugo smiled. "He'll have some stiff competition from the Andersons, but there's nothing wrong with that. The tourists will be the ones to benefit from it."

"I had lunch with Kyle yesterday," Abby continued. "He was able to track down Captain Zirka and checked him into a residential treatment program. There will be a job waiting for him with North Star Cruises when he's clean and sober."

Hugo nodded his approval. "Everything seems to be falling into place. By the way, I've been meaning to thank you for keeping me from making one of the biggest mistakes of my career."

"What's that?"

He smiled. "I think you know. My plan to hire Mick Wymore as a publicist for the conservatory. I'm sorry now that I even considered it."

"I still think hiring a publicist is a good idea. We've just seen the power of the press in action. Maybe we can use that power to do some good for the conservatory and the wildlife on Sparrow Island."

Hugo considered her words, then rose to his feet. "You may be right. I'll definitely give it some thought."

He headed toward the door, where he was met by Mary. They greeted each other, then Hugo let her pass through before he made his exit.

"This is a surprise," Abby said, noting her sister's new outfit. "It looks like you've been shopping."

Mary grinned. "I had to find something to go with my new bracelet." She held out her arm so Abby could see the wide wooden bracelet etched with orchids that Henry had given her along with the jewelry box.

"You look beautiful," Abby said.

"I bought a new outfit for you, too," Mary told her. "It's in the van."

"For me?" Abby checked her desk calendar to make sure she hadn't forgotten a special event. "What's the occasion?"

"Girls' night out," Mary replied. "I'm treating you to dinner at Winifred's. Margaret and Janet will be there too."

Margaret Blackstock and Janet Heinz were good friends of both of them. Abby had been so wrapped up in the orca case, she couldn't remember the last time they'd all gone out together.

Abby glanced down at her gray sweatshirt and jeans. "If we're going to Winifred's, I'll definitely need to change into something nicer than this."

Winifred's was the most elegant restaurant on Sparrow Island. Expensive, too.

"You'll love the outfit I picked out for you," Mary promised her. "A little different than your usual style, but I'm sure it will be perfect."

Abby trusted her judgment. Her sister had excellent taste in clothes. Besides, Abby was feeling a little adventurous today. A girls' night out sounded like fun.

Bobby appeared in the doorway, ready for his volunteer shift.

"Oh, I'm glad you're here too, Bobby," Mary cried, turning her wheelchair in his direction. "A letter arrived today from Lopez Island. And guess what? It's written in code."

Bobby's face lit up at Mary's news. "Yeah! We get to decipher another message."

They all gathered around Abby's desk as she distributed paper and pens to each of them. Then Mary set the coded message on the center of the desk.

Written in black ink on the message were a series of letters and numbers:

ZE1G2C2V4ZB1D2D2Z1ZN1D3T2Z1ZC2Q3G3Z
ZD2Q2E3F4Z1ZZ1Q2X3ZB1T2H3ZM4P2Y3J1V2G2H4Z
ZZ6P1ZV2J2F1ZX1G2F2H4J1P2K4Z
ZP1H2ZP3B1T2V3L4C2N2Q5ZD1Q2Y1Z
ZC2R4F2ZV2H3T1X5D3ZN1C2V4E2M5Z
ZV2K3M4T1ZG1T2L3F2B1Z1ZC2V2ZW3X1Q2Z
ZB1X4ZM1K2U1W3M1G2ZH2P4R3D1M2Z
ZF3J2Y4S1F3J2ZJ4K2P2T6F1J3B1P2Z
ZJ1V3ZK2Q3X2J1W3F1G3ZV2R3S4Z

"This is a long one," Mary said, scanning the paper. "Nine lines. It could take a while."

"Let's do what we did before," Abby suggested. "Except this time we'll each take three lines of the message and decode them. I'll take the first three lines. Mary, you can take the second three lines and Bobby can take the last three."

"Cool," Bobby exclaimed, ready for another decoding contest. He held his pencil at the ready, waiting until Mary and Abby did the same. "Ready . . . set . . . go!"

The only sound in the room was the hasty scribbling of pencils on paper.

"I've got mine done," Bobby announced.

He had to wait several minutes for Mary and Abby to catch up.

"Done!" the sisters said simultaneously.

Bobby shot his fist in the air in celebration. "I won again."

"Congratulations," Abby told him. "But you'll have to wait until last to tell us your portion of the message."

"Hurry," Mary prodded. "I want to know what it says."

Abby cleared her throat and read the first part of the message. "*Dear Abby Mary and Bobby you are invited to the wedding . . .*"

". . . *of Marshall Cox and Tessa March,*" Mary continued, reading her portion of the message, "*this Friday at two.*"

The sisters turned to Bobby to finish the message, though they both knew enough by now to make them smile with joy.

". . . *at Little Flock Church,*" Bobby read aloud, "*Finnegan is invited too.*"

Mary laughed. "Wait until Finnegan hears he's invited to a wedding. Looks like I'll have to go shopping for an appropriate outfit for him now."

Abby laughed with her. "I'm glad Tessa found her way home again." Then she reached over to squeeze her sister's hand. "And I'm so glad that I found my way home again too."

A NOTE FROM THE EDITORS

THIS ORIGINAL BOOK WAS created by the Books and Inspirational Media Division of Guideposts, the world's leading inspirational publisher. Founded in 1945 by Dr. Norman Vincent Peale and his wife Ruth Stafford Peale, Guideposts helps people from all walks of life achieve their maximum personal and spiritual potential. Guideposts is committed to communicating positive, faith-filled principles for people everywhere to use in successful daily living.

Our publications include award-winning magazines like *Guideposts*, *Angels on Earth*, *Sweet 16* and *Positive Thinking*, best-selling books, and outreach services that demonstrate what can happen when faith and positive thinking are applied to day-to-day life.

For more information, visit us online at www.guideposts.org, call (800) 431-2344 or write Guideposts, 39 Seminary Hill Road, Carmel, New York 10512.